IMPERSONATION

I0554307

Tamsin Walker

GARRETEER
PRESS

www.garreteerpress.com

Garreteer Press (UK)
www.garreteerpress.com

This novel is entirely a work of fiction. The names, characters, and incidents portrayed in it are the work of the author's imagination. Any resemblance to actual persons, living or dead, events or localities is entirely coincidental.

Book Layout © 'Spark' by Book Design Templates

Impersonation / Tamsin Walker 2nd Edition
First published by John Lynch Publishing 2012
978-1-9999318-0-3

For J and A

ONE

I caught a glimpse of myself today. Not the me of my mirror image, nor the me of my forgiving mind's eye, but the me that strangers see. I saw my description on the pages of a book, recognised myself in the words of a man I have never met.

I was on the train to work, looking by turns at the passing blur of the flatlands outside and the paperback on my lap, when I was overcome with a nagging feeling that something was amiss. Something unsettling had been said or done, but I had no idea what. I waited for it to either fade or crystallize, but it did neither. Instead, it lingered uncomfortably, following me off the train and taunting me throughout the halting bus ride to the shabby third-floor London office where I spend my time processing orders for hair restoration products.

It may have eluded me all day were it not for the ritual flirtations between my supervisor, Hazel, and Simon, who comes around selling lunchtime baguettes from a basket. I used to buy from him when I first started working here, but wasn't very good at the small talk in which he wraps his wares, so now I take a packed lunch instead. Hazel does not.

"I think I'll try the smoked turkey with pesto. And I'll have a blueberry muffin to go with it," she purred at him.

"All right darlin', anything for my favourite girl…"

"Will you have bagels tomorrow?"

"Sorry flower, I can't make it tomorrow. I've got to go to my auntie's funeral."

Funeral. The word hit me like a train speeding out of a long, unlit tunnel. My mind ran away without me, darting back through time, looking for the source of this sudden resonance. I picked through the remnants of last night's dreams and re-read the morning's newspaper headlines. Nowhere could I recall a funeral, so I replayed my journey to work, watching myself step into the busy carriage, find a seat and silently debate whether or not to take off my coat. I eavesdropped anew on the hushed chat of commuters around me and re-opened my bag to see if it held any clues. The paperback felt relevant to my search. At least vaguely. So, while Hazel continued to play coy with Simon, I opened it anew.

*T*his story, Dear Reader, begins one summer not so very long ago, on a train filled with office workers and the heavy odour of their collective August existence. Among them were three scantily clad girls who wore their rude rolls of fat with misplaced pride, and through whose poorly painted lips came unsavoury breath telling unsavoury tales of their sexual conquests of the night before.

A middle-aged woman listened with envy to their lurid bragging as delirium tremens lay siege to her body. Mentally breaking her vow of sobriety, she sulkily mouthed the words 'make mine a double' at a boy perched on his father's pin-striped trousers across the aisle. The child stared back at her with wide-eyed fear, brightening only when his young eyes hit upon a bald man whose stomach was oozing from the gaps between the buttons of his inadequate shirt.

The ample man acknowledged the child with a wink and sought to entertain it by blowing his nose into a piece of newspaper. The father struggled to conceal his disgust, and repositioned the boy to face a younger, haughty-looking woman who, refusing to be drawn by any of what she saw, carefully smoothed the folds of the cream and green floral print dress she would be wearing to the funeral she would happily soon be planning.

There it was, the source of the resonance. The mental relief was blissful, and I closed the book and leaned back in my chair to enjoy this victory over my sluggish memory. But the triumph was short-lived, because something was still not right. Whatever it was, that something appeared to be connected to the book now lying face down on top of a stack of papers on my desk. I tried to ignore it but the blurb on the back cover rose to meet me.

'The Ruthlessness of One Man' is based on the physical appearance of a real-life London commuter. Perhaps she is sitting across from you, at your side, or is the one you just walked past. Perhaps she is even you. Whoever she is, Mr Walden's interpretation of her life will leave you, Dear Reader, in no doubt that things are rarely as they seem.

I received *The Ruthlessness of One Man*, as a loyalty gift from the old-fashioned book club I joined a few years ago and had previously never heard of either it or its author, Mr Walden. But it held a certain appeal, so rather than dedicate another lunch hour to helping what appears to be an endless number of balding men – and some women - I read.

It was hot inside the compartment, and although she felt it too, Davina had no intention of joining the chorus of predictable heat-induced moans and groans. She rolled her green eyes at her fellow passengers' futile attempts to fan away the inhospitable heat, mentally berating them for fuelling the very furnaces they were at pains to extinguish whilst simultaneously spreading the ghastly human smells that assaulted her every intake of breath. These she filtered by holding to her nose a crumpled lace-trim handkerchief. Each time she did so, she bowed her head just enough for her fine shoulder-length red hair to fall forward and reveal a thin pink scar below her left ear.

I think I am that woman.

I'm not given to vanity, but the likenesses were too great in number to be coincidental. I read the words again with deliberation, checking them against the facts of my life, and asking reason to guide me to my senses. It stressed that of all the commuters in the country, I am not the kind to stand out and inspire writers to their pens. I may have shoulder-length red hair, which is sometimes so fine I've considered buying the products we sell, but so do thousands of other women. I also have a cream and green floral print dress, but I know for a fact I'm not alone in that either. Green eyes are hardly unique, and even scars are not hard to come by. But when it came to the line about the crumpled lace-trim handkerchief, reason reached a dead-end, and left me there.

How many of these nameless, faceless women bound together by the unity of their haircuts, dresses and accidents are also comforted by the smell of rose oil bled into a small square of lacy cotton?

"Enjoying yourself?"

I slam the book shut and look up to find a pair of pale blue eyes staring at me from the depths of a puffy pink face.

"Oh, you gave me a fright."

"So I see. Good book?"

Hazel has an absurdly keen interest in my life. I never give much away; in part because it would never stay with her, but also because the reality would disappoint her. Perhaps even more than it disappoints me.

"I've only just started it."

"What's it about?"

She tries to snatch the book from my hands but I pull it away, accidentally scraping one of her fingers with my badly clipped thumbnail in the process.

"Ouch! What was that for? I only wanted a look."

"I'm sorry. I hope I didn't hurt you."

Hazel studies the wound which is barely managing to bleed, and sucks on it with a pained expression. Without another word, she rolls on her chair back to her desk and rummages through her top drawer. After a moment, she shouts a general plea into the room.

"Anyone got a bandage?"

Hypochondria is the oil on the wheels of Hazel's day. The temp from the reception desk hurries to her aid with a box of assorted plasters.

"Ooo, that looks sore. What did you do?"

Hazel strokes her expensive white blonde curls and flashes me a reproachful glance.

"Ruth scratched me." She looks over at me again, her drawn-on eyebrows raised. "Makes me think you must have something to hide."

I shove the book into my back pocket, wishing I'd scratched her a little bit harder.

Our toilets are not a place I like to spend more than the bare minimum of time - they have a cold, institutional acridity about them. The cracked seats are invariably spattered with pee that other women can't be bothered to wipe away, the bowls are stained, and the ancient toilet brushes are themselves too soiled to be of any sanitary use. But the stench neutralizes eventually, and at least here, I'm alone.

I pored over the back cover again, shifting between believing and disbelieving that I could really be the real-life London commuter to which Mr Walden refers.

On the inside cover I find an acknowledgement.

I dedicate my book to the beautiful face which inspired me to write it. In a railway carriage full of people, she stood out and arrested the attention of my thoughts and my pen. I thank her for showing me the truth, and hope she will like the life I have imagined for her.

When I read that, disbelief conquers belief. Fact is, I'm far too dowdy to stand out in a group of three, much less an entire railway carriage. Nothing about me is beautiful or has the power to arrest anyone's attention. There must be a greater likelihood of my winning the lottery. And I don't even play.

- 2 -

I've been trying to put *The Ruthlessness of One Man* out of my mind all afternoon, but it just won't leave me alone. A little voice keeps whispering to me that I've lost out to another woman who shares some of my features and dresses like me, but who wears them both with greater flair. Whoever she is, she has "arrested my attention", too, so when Hazel is happily occupied with a packet of custard creams and her regulation pot of afternoon tea, I return to Mr Walden and his muse.

There is a long section in which he describes his leading lady's dislike of other people, a characteristic he attributes to her "difficult circumstances", although he does not indicate what they might be. I'm aware that I'd like to know more, but don't stop to think about it for more than a second, because my eye has moved down the page and come to rest on something more relevant.

> *When the train arrived at its destination, Davina remained in her seat while the masses, to which she felt she did not belong, spewed onto the platform. Not until the last of her fellow passengers had left the carriage, did she get up, put her worn black satchel over her shoulder, and step outside into London town where, unbeknownst to her, her story began.*

To the careless eye, the description could easily have been overlooked. But mine is keen, and tells me that the protagonist now not only has my hair, my scarf, my dress and my handkerchief, she also has my black satchel. What's more, she does as I do when arriving in London on my morning commute, and waits until the train has emptied before getting off.

Fear and excitement gallop over me, waking my nerves from their shallow sleep and pushing me to race through the text for further references to make my case, and give life to my life. Could it really be about me?

Yes, Dear Reader, Davina's story began where it began, but would end elsewhere. It would end at the other end of the country, in what some describe as another country. It would end more happily than it began. For we met Davina as a loner; a sad woman of thirty years who trudged rather than tripped through life, as blind to its reality as a common garden mouldywarp to everything but the blackness through which it tunnels.

Mouldywarp, I have just found out, means mole.

What Davina and the mouldywarp did not have in common, however, was determination. Indeed, this was a characteristic which the former lacked in spades, and the lack did not serve her well. Had she been more indomitable, she might have found her way alone, and without having to refer to any books for guidance. But as it was, books were her only real friends, the only things she could truly rely upon for company and comfort. And she was in great need of both.

You see, Dear Reader, Davina had been born into a life that had tugged down the corners of her mouth until it had engraved sadness into the smooth skin of her delicate face. It was a life so sad that it had never given her anything to smile about; a life so devoid of smiles that she didn't stop to question whether she should be asking more of her days than waking, working, and sleeping. Happily, however, although she did not know it on the morning she arrived at Liverpool Street Station wearing her cream and green dress, she was about to meet someone who would answer the question for her.

My train goes to and from Liverpool Street. And I do love books. But I don't love this one. The prose is beyond purple and I don't see how my appearance could lead Mr Walden to think I am a sad person in need of company and comfort. I have Paul for company and comfort. Besides that, I smile as much as anyone else.

Although well-read, Davina had never received any kind of induction into classical music. If she listened to music at all, it was to the variety that has sugar as its substance and coating, and that was not acceptable. So, when she received an anonymous invitation to attend Bach's Mass in B Minor in one of London's finest churches, Davina instinctively understood she had to accept.

When she arrived at the sacred edifice and passed through the wooden door into the vast sacred space soon to be filled with the majesty of the music, she felt naked. She could hide nothing there; not from Jesus or his disciples blazing blue from their places in the windows, the musicians tuning their instruments, or the hundreds of people squeezed onto the dark wooden pews.

She might, Dear Reader, have given in to the powerful urge to leave, were it not for her desire to meet whoever had issued the invitation. She had not been in the nave for more than a matter of minutes before she was approached by a most attractive silver-haired older gentleman who silently ushered her into a back row pew, where he proceeded to sit beside her.

Shoulders brushing, they shared a programme with the shy intimacy of strangers. Twice she opened her mouth to ask him if he was the man to whom she owed her thanks for being there, but twice she was silenced by the graceful way he moved his right hand in time to the music. And twice she was overcome with the certainty that this man, whoever he was, would look magnificent on her arm, and even more so standing upon the greatest of all the world's pedestals, skilfully weaving his musicians through the timeless beauty of Johann Sebastian Bach.

I don't know whether to laugh or cry. If this is about me, and I'm torn between thinking it is and knowing it isn't, I must give off the air of an uneducated woman who's waiting to be carried away by an awe-inspiring stranger with silver hair and a thing for Bach.

> *The day after the concert, Davina was preparing for a visit from her married Thursday night lover when the telephone rang.*
>
> *"Good morning dear"*
>
> *"Hello, who is this?"*
>
> *"Please forgive me for taking such a liberty. We met at the concert last night, and I wanted to say how much I enjoyed sitting with you…"*
>
> *Davina knew instantly who she was speaking to.*
>
> *"… and that it was a great pleasure to meet you."*
>
> *"I… how did you get my telephone number?"*
>
> *"That doesn't matter, I think we should just rejoice in the fact that I have managed to find you."*
>
> *"But…"*
>
> *"I would greatly like to have the opportunity to deepen our acquaintance, and would suggest that we meet at the entrance to the British Library at half past noon."*
>
> *"I'm afraid I'll be working today Mr…"*
>
> *"Is it not your custom to break from your duties at noon?"*
>
> *"Yes, but…"*
>
> *"In that case there can be no problem."*
>
> *Davina was itching to know how the mysterious man with the dark eye brows and well-defined bone structure had managed to get hold of her telephone number, and how he knew when she took her lunch break. Yes, Dear Reader, she was itching to know. And in the fullness of time she will find out. Just as she will learn all about the connection between Bach's B Minor and the funeral that she will initially deem inappropriate, but later help plan down to the tiniest, finest detail.*

I've read enough to understand that my face did not inspire Mr Walden to think good of me. Quite the opposite. He seems to have hollowed me out and filled me with stupidity, loneliness, and something frightening I can't put my finger on.

And it doesn't stop there. As I read on, it becomes clear that the person whose funeral Davina – whoever she might be – will delight in preparing is a woman called Shelagh. Mr Walden makes it clear that Davina only pretends to care about the deceased. He has her consumed by a fake loss, and sinks her into a morass of misery, which she smears all over her face lest anybody, stranger or otherwise, be left in doubt as to the extent of her suffering. She becomes an image of wanton woe, and revels in it without actually feeling it. Under Mr Walden's pen, she turns the deceased's end into her own curtain call. She carries her sadness everywhere she goes, and adds to the overall effect by being carefully careless with appearance. Until that is, the day of the funeral itself.

Like a dying general, Davina will rally her troops in her hour of need, and she will leave them to deal with her despair while she turns her mind to the more pressing issue of her funeral outfit, because she will be determined to be the belle of this burial ball.

Early on Friday morning, which is when the funeral will take place, she will bathe in luxury salts, and slip into a pair of silk stockings and a cream and green dress. She will stop to wonder if Shelagh can see them together, planning for their shared future in which she will not even have a supporting role.

She will then sit in front of the mirror, practising looks of sorrow. Once happy with her sombre pout, dressed and made-up, she will drench her lace-trim handkerchief in enough perfume to ensure her eyes water when she holds it up to them, and will take her place in the church where Bach's mass will be playing.

He will not expect her to hold the eulogy, but will do so himself with far greater anguish than is fitting for the woman in the box. He will cling to the pulpit so hard that it almost threatens to collapse under his weight. But that will be nothing, it will become clear, compared to his emotional display in the churchyard.

Kneeling so far over the freshly dug grave that he will almost fall on top of the coffin, he will claw at the dark soil which form the walls of Shelagh's new home, howling as he does so at the injustice of his loss and at his future, which will see him struggling on alone with nothing but a broken heart for company.

"This isn't a library, you know, Ruth."

Hazel has biscuit crumbs on her face, and looks like a chubby child as she extends the packet to me.

"How's my report coming on?"

"I'm getting there."

"Doesn't look like it. You won't get it finished with your nose in a book."

"I just had to check something."

"Oh you did, did you?"

She withdraws the packet of biscuit, takes one, and puts it in her mouth.

"I really don't want to have to play the part of a slave-driving boss here, Ruth, but if you insist on reading when you're supposed to be working, you're hardly going to leave me with any choice. Are you?"

As she speaks, she spits bits of masticated custard creams at me. One little blob lands on my nose, where it feels as though it is burning a hole in my skin. I wipe it away with the back of my sleeve, making a mental note to put my jumper in the washing machine when I get home, and turn my attention to my computer screen, hoping she will go away, so I can digest what I've just read. But she's not leaving. Her heavy frame hovers around me.

"Don't know what you see in books. Magazines are much better."

There's something distasteful about Hazel. It's not just the way she chews, but the fact that everything from her hair to her kindness, when she can be bothered, is fake. Yet she manages to sell it as the real deal.

"That's where you get all the juicy details about celebrities' sex lives."

With no forewarning her naked thighs barge into the frame of my mind. She's using them to straddle an anonymous man. I screw up my eyes to squeeze the image away. When it's gone, I straighten my back and begin banging at my keyboard like I really mean it. I don't see the words I'm typing; the screen is blurred by questions and answers chasing one another around my mind. Is it me? Could it be me? Surely not. How? Impossible. But if, then why me? Why would Mr Walden want to borrow my physical appearance to attach to a schemer like Davina? Do I look so cold-hearted and devious? Why did he choose me? Did he choose me? How many women really have my scar and my handkerchief? My satchel? My commute to Liverpool Street?

My palms are sticky.

When Hazel is out of the room, I go back to the book, my eyes riding roughshod over the small print on the inside front cover. It says no more about the author than that he and his grown-up daughter live in southern England, and that this is his debut work of fiction. The scant publishing details link him to a Dragonfly Press. I run a search and find the publisher's address along with a line instructing members of the public wishing to get in touch with authors to use their electronic form to do so.

To: A.Young@DFPress.co.uk
From: RMorton@BaldNoMore.co.uk
Subject: The Ruthlessness of One Man by Mr Walden

Dear Mr Walden,

I am writing to inform you that in reading your book 'The Ruthlessness of One Man', I came face to face with an image of myself. I don't mean that I had a revelatory moment of identification with your character, but that I believe I am the woman upon whom you based your protagonist. This is a most unusual situation to find myself in and, frankly, it isn't very pleasant. I am not happy that you have seen fit to use my appearance in this way, and feel I deserve an explanation. Please contact me at this email address as soon as possible.

Yours sincerely,

Ruth Morton

I send the mail and try to turn back to my work, but my powers of concentration are locked inside the pages of *The Ruthlessness of One Man*. It occurs to me now that the title is filled with potential for interpretation. But I don't wear my name on my bag or my coat, and I never answer my phone with "this is Ruth Morton", so reassure myself that that, at least, can be nothing other than a coincidence.

"Ruth, I don't know what's got into you today."

For the shortest of moments, I consider coming clean and telling Hazel about my possible discovery.

"Every time I look over at you, you're either reading or dreaming."

How I wish I could tell her to shut up.

"Have you gone deaf?"

I want to be somewhere else. Anywhere but here under the glare of Hazel's scavenging eye and our fluorescent office strips.

"Ruth? I'm talking to you."

"I'm not feeling well," I hear myself say. I don't know where my words are taking me, but I'm glad of their intervention, and follow them blindly.

"You were all right a moment ago."

"Actually, I wasn't."

I'm trembling now, and I put my hands on the desk so she can see it. I don't care if she sacks me. I only care about getting out of this office in which Mr Walden suddenly looms so large. I need to return to the relative safety of existence as I knew it this morning, and the only way to do that is to go home.

*

On the platform a monotone voice announces the delay in departure time of my train, and for a welcome moment I'm surrounded by the familiar unified groan of commuters who'd been hoping, like me, to get out of the city ahead of the rush.

"What the bloody hell is it this time?"

I turn around just in time to see the suited man to my left closing his mouth around the word 'time'. Is he talking to me? He's looking right at me as if he knows me. I lower my gaze, but he continues his disgruntled talk about trains and delays, inching closer to me as he speaks. A couple of people look over towards him, seconding his incredulity with approving grunts and nods. I say nothing, but still he stares directly at me. Why doesn't he turn to the other passengers, to the ones who share his annoyance? As I ask myself that question, I come up with an answer that plunges my heart to the pit of my stomach. He might have recognised me. He might have read Mr Walden's book and seen me in it.

I can feel the colour spreading like a bushfire up my neck, burning into my face and making my scar stand out. I try to hide it by repositioning my hair, undeniably thin and red. I move down the platform, looking no one in the eye, but I swear I can feel their stares pressing into my back as I search for a corner in which to wait for the train alone.

I'm reminded of a nightdress my mother wore when she was a child. The first time she put it on, I thought it was a summer dress and much too pretty to wear to bed, but she did so anyway, and I accepted it for what it was. But then, one hot day when she wore it to go to the beach, I was certain everyone was staring at her, judging her for not bothering to get dressed. This time, it's me they are judging.

- 3 -

He can see her house and he knows she's in it now. She came home early today, and he wonders if she is ailing. He watches her move around inside her front room, seemingly unable to set her mind to anything. He sees her sit, yet not relax, in the armchair by the window, drum the fingers of her left hand on its arm before getting back up, walking to, and fiddling with the vase of wilting pink roses on the table. He observes her leave the room only to return a moment later with a glass of water she does not drink, but puts on a shelf beside which she now stands. She picks up a remote control, switches on the television set, lies on the sofa, and covers herself with a blanket.

He notes that she looks wan. On the whole he has no time for illness, which he is convinced is a sign of weakness. That being so, he would like to believe that his thoughts about her physical state are coloured by the crossword he delivered earlier in the week on the theme of poor health. But when he sees her put her hand to her forehead, he wonders if she is feverish, *Eternity in a cod for example – that's a few degrees ov*er *(8)*. Or perhaps she just has a common cold, P*ublic land which is rarely warm. It's viral (6,4)*. He would like to tell her to check for herself. He knows she has a thermometer, *Nothing to link gas and linear measures in this mercurial device (11)*.

He will be watching the details of her behaviour for the rest of the evening to determine her physical state, and whether he can give her a clean bill of health, *Medical verdict when spotless William removes nothing from the loofah mix (5,4,2,6)* or whether she is a sick as a dog, *Poorly like a Venetian boss who's lost his bottom? Or just plain fed up (4,2,1,3)*.

- 4 -

I don't like the name Davina. I've disliked it ever since Davina Rawlins moved into the house along the track where my mother still lives. She was two years older than me and quickly singled me out as easy prey for her devious, manipulative games. I was wary of her from the first time I set eyes on her, and quickly grew accustomed to lowering my head whenever I saw her coming. But my resistance to her company was matched in equal measure by her pointed interest in mine, and one day when I came out of school, she was waiting for me.

"Your mum said you can come to mine for tea."

There was nothing I wanted less than to go to her house, and I was horrified with my mother for encouraging this mismatch. Powerless to resist, I followed her to her home where she lured me into an uneasy friendship with a plastic bag full of technicoloured Cindy doll clothes she insisted I take home with me. What I didn't realise was that in accepting Davina's offering, I had unconsciously signed a contract to play mouse to her cat.

The next morning, she rang my doorbell, inviting me to walk to school with her. Ignoring my pleading look to be rescued by an adult excuse, my mother smiled and sent me on my way. For the five minutes we walked in tandem, Davina explained to me what we would be doing after school that day. We would go to my house and she would distract my mother while I would steal one pound 20 pence from her purse, which she would then spend on a stuffed dog she had set her heart on. If I dared to tell anyone, she would, she assured me, make sure that many forms of danger came my way. It was the first in a long line of threats which drove me to beg, borrow, and steal to satisfy her every whim and thus save myself from one of countless potentially ugly fates.

I dreamed of that Davina last night. She had her trademark long black hair but, apart from that, she looked like me. She was sitting on a train holding a book. I woke in a disoriented sweat, and spent the rest of the night wide awake, my limbs growing ever stiffer with the ache of tiredness.

I'm still thinking of Davina, both Davinas, as I join the scrum to board the train to work this morning. A man smiles right into my face, like he knows me, though I am sure he doesn't. He turns back to look at me again as he walks past, and again he smiles. No one smiled at me like that yesterday. I would remember.

I find a seat, but my conscience chases me out of it when I catch sight of an elderly woman clinging unsteadily to the back of someone's headrest. I give her my place and join the cluster of bodies near the doors. The smell of sleep clings to someone near me and I look down so as not to have to breathe it in. My flat black slip-ons look dull compared to the elegant heels beside them and I am willing to believe for a blissful second, that I cannot be Walden's Davina. Other women with better shoes would be better suited for the role. But he did not make any mention of shoes, but of dresses, hair, scars, bags, books, stations and handkerchiefs. My stomach calls out for food it couldn't digest.

I wonder if Walden is anywhere on this train, possibly in this very carriage. His shoes could be the ones next to the heels. Or they could be at the window, tapping while he fills notebooks with slanderous musings about his next victim.

I'm bumped out of my thoughts by a nudge from behind me. I stiffen immediately. My instincts tell me to turn around and see where it came from, but I fight them and stare straight ahead, pretending to be oblivious.

It happens again. Not so much a nudge this time as a tap. A definite, purposeful tap on my back. I stand still as the certainty that it must be Mr Walden or someone who has read his book spreads to the tips of my fingers and the pit of my stomach.

I want to turn around, but my legs won't allow it. So I stand still. Rigid and blushing wildly. Droplets of sweat run from my armpits down the side of my torso, making even my own body seem like my enemy.

Another nudge.

In my mind I have already turned, while in reality I remain rooted to the spot.

"Now you do it."

The voice behind me is unfamiliar. Female. Young.

"No, it was your idea,' hisses another.

"Still your turn."

"Yeah…go on."

Out of nowhere I feel a thud right in the centre of my back. My self-preservation instinct takes hold and I spin round to see two teenage girls feebly trying not to laugh. A third looks as shocked as I feel. She offers me an apology before being dragged back into the intimate world of infectious giggling she shares with her friends. I'm still looking at them when the tallest of the three flicks her pink-streaked hair out of her face, stops laughing and glares at me.

"What are you staring at? She said she's sorry. She didn't do it on purpose."

"Okay," is all I can get out, before turning back to face the collection of eyes now fixed on me from all over the carriage. Behind me the girls continue to laugh. The sound of them takes me back to high school, to a time when I was too young and inexperienced to recognise my body's warning signs, to the gym class when my period announced itself to all and sundry by trickling unmistakeably down the inside of my left leg. I instinctively press my thighs together. But the other passengers are looking at my face, not my legs. They are sizing me up, asking themselves and each other what just happened. I am asking myself the same thing.

The conductor announces that the train will shortly be arriving at the next station, I don't hear the name, but it doesn't matter, because wherever it is, I'm getting off.

For the three long minutes it takes to get there, I pray to a God in whom I'm not sure I believe that the girls will not push me again. My prayers are answered and, when the train comes to a halt, I squeeze past the other passengers with as much dignity as I can muster, climb off and cross the platform. I am going home.

- 5 -

Morna Morton rose with the Hebridean sun and came down the stairs of her little cottage to make breakfast and lay the table for the walkers she could already hear stirring above her. With the deft hands of experience, she poached kippers, made tea, cut thick slices from the bread she'd baked the night before, and set it all out on the kitchen table. She had a new arrival due in around midday, which gave her a couple of hours to lick Ruth's old room back into shape. She'd as soon not have to share her home with strangers, but she had no other choice. Her pension covered her daily needs but wasn't enough to put anything by, and she had been sufficiently thrown about by life to understand the importance of a little something under the mattress.

Today's guest was no ordinary visitor. He was not coming to hike or to pray, but to help her. He had come up from London late yesterday, but had opted to spend a night in Oban before coming on to her. He wasn't the first to do that, although it was a mystery to her why anyone would want to spend a moment longer on the mainland when they could be walking among the rocks and angels of the tiny island where she had first sought refuge exactly thirty-three years ago. Oban had a folly; Iona had an abbey. Oban had views of the islands; Iona was an island. There was no contest in her eyes.

She had everything planned for his visit, and had washed her best crockery, polished her best cutlery, and pressed her best linen accordingly. She had bought in real coffee and a more expensive bottle of single malt than her budget could comfortably allow, ordered a good cut of beef, and made one of her legendary apple crumbles.

And when they weren't eating, she would guide him around the island, leaving him in no doubt whatsoever that there is a place on earth where the heavens descend so far that it is possible to see inside. She felt it might go some way to explaining why she was taking what she knew to be an unusual course of action.

- 6 -

It's 11.55 and I've been home for almost three hours. In that time I've checked my inbox dozens of times for a reply from the publisher, but so far there has been nothing besides a few lines from Hazel to say she hopes I feel better soon but that I am contractually bound to phone rather than mail in when I am sick.

I've searched for Mr Walden and any reviews of his work, but have so far failed to find a single reference to him. His book is on the table in front of me. I know I have to keep reading if I want to be able to make a case when the publishers do finally respond, but the prospect is daunting. I remind myself that even though Walden has used my face to draw his protagonist, the story he has inserted me into is fictional.

I take a deep breath and go back to where I left off.

When Davina arrived at the entrance to the British Library for the meeting, it was to find her companion for the day awaiting her. She was immediately struck by the stylish cut of his suit and careful way in which he had slicked back his hair. Their combined effect lent him an air of youthfulness she found entirely pleasing. Had she been a religious woman she might have thanked the divine for this intervention in her lonely life, but she wasn't, so she inwardly thanked him for taking the initiative.

"Hello dear, I'm delighted you were able to join me."
"As am I."
"Would you like to sit?"
"Aren't we going inside?"

"I've already been in, and would now like to enjoy the fresh air.."

Davina sat down beside the handsome stranger, who smiled at her fondly.

"Would you like to know why I suggested we meet here?"

"Yes, I would."

"Because I know how much you love books."

"Yes I do. But how do you know that, Mr... it is rather embarrassing for me, but I'm afraid I don't know your name."

"No, not embarrassing at all. You don't yet know it because I've yet to divulge it."
"I see. Might you now?"

"I'm afraid not my dear. You see I make it a habit of not revealing my name to anyone until I know them a little better. I find people make too many judgements based upon names. Don't you agree?"

"I don't know."

"Trust me my dear, they do. Take your name, for instance, it makes me think of people I don't like, so I choose to call you Davina instead. Davina is such a pretty name, don't you agree? It means you are loved. Which you are."

"Am I?"

"More than you know. But let us return to the matter in hand. Let us return to your love of books. I wanted to sit here with you where we could both be close to our beloved."

The gentleman put his hand on Davina's knee.

"And on that note, I have something for you."

He handed her a small parcel, which she opened with the care of one who was not in the habit of receiving gifts. She undid the ribbon and let the paper around it fall away to reveal a book entitled 'The Ruthlessness of One Man' by Mr Walden.

I stumble over these lines, aware that the information they contain is the kind I would like in a book were my own face, name and sanity not at stake. My eyes move down the page with caution.

> *"Thank you. I've never read this one."*
> *"I know."*
> *"Have you?" Davina asked him, her Scottish accent padding out her vowels.*

I am Scottish. And I am no longer in any doubt. I am Davina. Davina is me.

My computer beeps at me with the sound of incoming mail. I open my account, hoping that whatever awaits me is from the man behind my alternative incarnation. There is one message from an address I don't recognise - A.Young @DFPress - and the subject line reads *The Ruthlessness of One Man*. My heart powers into a sprint as I click it open.

To: RMorton@BaldNoMore.co.uk
From: A.Young@DFPress.co.uk
Subject: The Ruthlessness of One Man by Mr Walden

Dear Ruth Morton,

I am writing in response to your mail requesting we put you in touch with a writer named Mr Walden. I'm sorry to have to inform you, however, we do not work with anyone of that name and do not have a book called 'The Ruthlessness of One Man' on our list. I'm sorry we cannot be of greater assistance to you, but we wish you best of luck in your continued search.

Best

Alex Young

This can't be.

Of all my potential scenarios, this was not one of them. There must be a mistake. How can they never have heard of him, when a copy of a book bearing both Mr Walden's name and that of their company is right here in front of me? Maybe they're protecting his identity. This Alex Young could have forwarded my mail to Walden, who then real-ised he'd been caught out and, not wanting to face the consequences, asked them to cover for him. Coward.

An image of Walden as a stubby man with a greying moustache and greasy hair forms before me. I'm standing in front of him, taller than he, but made taller still by the smallness of his position. I will find you, Mr Walden, and when I do, you had better have a good reason for all of this.

Without really thinking about what I'm going to say, I dial the number at the bottom of the mail.

"Good morning, Dragonfly Press."

"I'd like to speak to Alex Young."

"I'll put you through. Can I take your name?"

I give it to her and my ear is immediately flooded with a few tinny bars of Beethoven's Moonlight Sonata.

"Hello, can I help you?" a voice cuts in. I had assumed Alex Young would be a man.

"Oh, erm hello, my name is Ruth Morton. I wrote to you last night trying to track down an author called Mr Walden."

"I just sent you a mail about that. If you check your in-box."

"I know. Thing is, it's critical that I get in touch with him."

"As I said, I'm not familiar with either author or title."

"Could you put me through to someone who is?"

"I don't think you understand. Dragonfly Press has never published a book by anyone called Mr Walden, nor has it published a title called *The Ruthlessness of One Man*."

My mouth is dry. She must know more than she is telling me.

"But I have the book right here… It's a thin book. The front cover shows a photograph of a train carriage. And it clearly says it's published by Dragonfly Press. You are Dragonfly Press, aren't you?"

"Yes, we are."

"Then how do you explain the fact that the book I'm holding bears the name of your company?"

"I can't… I'm afraid it's a mystery to me."

As the publisher's well-rounded vowels sound on, my doorbell rings. I try to keep listening to her, but my attention has been split down the middle.

"You could try America."

America? The bell rings a second time. I get up, but before I can walk to the door, the possibility of the caller being Walden has risen in me and forced me back down.

"I know of at least one publisher there called Dragon-fly."

"I don't think… I mean, are you sure…"

"Good luck in your search."

She puts the phone down before I can say goodbye. I still have the receiver pressed to my ear when the person at my front door raps on the wood. I sit perfectly still, waiting for whoever it is to go away, but his or her persistence matches my own. Nerves prick at my palms as I hear the gravel around my doorstep being ground underfoot. In my rational mind, I know it can't be Mr Walden because he doesn't know where I live, but my irrational side says the feet doing the grinding belong to a stout man with a moustache. He knocks again, pounding out a tune on my front door. Why are we waiting… at least that's what it sounds like. I remain as still as still until I eventually hear the sound of his feet retreat in defeat.

I run upstairs to my bedroom and hide behind the velvet curtains to get a view of my departing visitor. It's a man. Not the stout one I'd imagined, but a tall, unfamiliar one. He strides confidently away from my door and rounds the corner at the top of the path, only to vanish behind the unruly hedge that shields me from prying eyes. It withholds everything but a glance at his profile. I will him to turn around so I can see him face-on, but he ignores my silent petition and marches down the road with a confidence of someone who has made the journey before.

At the door I look for traces of his identity, or a note on the mat, but draw a blank. I open the door and look outside but find nothing there either. Nothing but the faint scent of aftershave, which if his, would tell me that the mystery caller is not a man of expensive taste.

- 7 -

He has had a confusing day today. It got off to an unprom-
ising start when he realised she had left for work without
taking his book with her. His spirits rose, however, when
she unexpectedly returned home less than two hours later
and soon thereafter picked up the volume in question and
began to read.

He would have liked her to spend a little longer at it
than she had, but put her distraction down to the unwanted
caller who knocked at her door with such impertinent insistence. Ever since that episode, which he was happy to
note had not ended favourably for the visitor, he could tell
she had not been herself.

He wondered again if she might be sickening and, although he did not wish her to be, he reminded himself that,
if sick, she might be inclined to break the date he is certain
she has made for tonight. It is the night of the week that her
wedded friend – he knows his name is Paul, but prefers to
call him Thor for obvious reasons – invariably comes calling. He does not like Thor, and does not like her to spend
time with him.

If Thor does come, he will do so, as he always does at
eight. He will bring her a bunch of flowers, *Blooms as distinguished chap hides German lion? (7),* and a bottle of
wine, *Mayfair, or thereabouts, north east. Vintage stuff!
(4).* White. And unbeknownst to her, while she is still upstairs applying unnecessary make-up to her perfect
features, Thor will glance to the left and right before removing his wedding band and pressing her doorbell.

Even though she keeps time well and knows enough of Thor to be sure he will be there on the stroke of eight, she will jump a little, as she always does when she hears him ring. She will then, increasing the pace of her movements, fold back the bed covers, spray some lemon scent into the air, and close the curtains to the watching world. She will go downstairs, where she and Thor will sip their wine, gradually inching together until they are kissing. After a few moments, they will adjourn to the bedroom to copulate, *New couple at it, indeed (8),* before returning two, or sometimes three hours later, so that Thor can collect his briefcase. Before he leaves, he will give her a stiff hug goodbye.

He longs for the day this will all change, for the day she realises she does not need this pretend romance, *After some gym Romeo adds gas to make present for a lady? (7)*, because she belongs both with and to him. Once she has read the book, she will understand that he is the only man she needs in her life, and will be overjoyed to have someone trustworthy at the centre of her existence. He is imagining that future when he catches sight of Thor parking his fast car at the top of the street.

- 8 -

My unsatisfactory exchange with the Alex Young has been pawing at me all day long. I have turned and turned it in my mind, but there is no angle from which it makes sense. The Dragonfly logo on the book matches the one on the publisher's website, as does the font of their name.

Just for the sake of it, and without expecting to turn anything up, I run a search for American publishing houses of the same name. I come up with two. One is in Chicago, but it only deals with poetry, and the other, which is in Oklahoma, specialises in philosophical texts. I fleetingly wonder whether there is any way *The Ruthlessness of One Man* could possibly be deemed philosophical, but conclude there is not. It has a genre of its own: gratuitous slander.

Every time I think of Walden having his version of me feign sadness at the death of this Shelagh woman, fury grapples with fear inside me. And as I go upstairs to get ready for Paul's visit, I ask myself over and over again, how, by simply looking at me, the author could have spun such an elaborate tale of selfishness and heartlessness. Is that how other people perceive me? Is that what my face invites them to think?

The doorbell rings. It always makes me jump. I quickly fold back the covers on the bed and spray some lemon scent into the air above it. Paul likes lemons, and I'm more generous with the bottle than usual in the hope he will succumb to the freshness and break his self-imposed rule of never staying the night. I don't want to be alone tonight. As the bell rings for a second time, I close the curtains and hurry downstairs to let him in.

The first half hour is always awkward, but tonight I'm tenser and clumsier than usual. It's hard to imagine that before the evening is out he will have been on top of me, me perhaps on him, the two of us side by side, and I will have seen everything that is currently still buttoned and zipped inside his shirt and suit.

He's loosening his tie and has begun moving closer to me on the sofa. It'll be another few minutes before his fingers reach for mine and several more before our lips touch. Until this moment I'd thought I'd be silent on my role in Mr Walden's book, but now he's this close, I know I'm not going to be able to concentrate on him and us until I've shared my experiences of the past two days.

I start by explaining the premise of *The Ruthlessness of One Man*, but don't immediately tell him I think the physical description can be traced back to me. I'm afraid he might think me vain or arrogant or paranoid, or perhaps all three. So after setting the scene, I say I think it's morally questionable to do as Mr Walden has done.

Paul doesn't agree. He thinks it a clever way to attract public attention.

His praise for something in which I am involved warms me to him and to myself. But not to the book, and once the glow has faded, I want him to join me in my loathing of it and the liberties it takes.

"Don't you think it's wrong to take someone's physical appearance and fill it with a different personality?"

"No. And anyway, I bet he just made up a physical description and said it was based on a real person."

"What would be the point of that?"

"Could be a good marketing strategy."

"I don't see how."

"You clearly don't watch television."

"I do sometimes."

"In that case you'd know that every woman and her Chihuahua wants a share of the limelight..."

I don't see what that has to do with the book, but his tone makes me think I ought to, and I don't want to seem foolish by admitting otherwise.

"…and that if someone writes a book about a real person, people are going to buy it to see if they're the one the character is based on."

"But I didn't even know it was based on a real person until after I'd started reading it."

"In that case you illustrate my point perfectly."

"What point?"

"That everyone wants to stand out in one way or another."

"I don't follow."

"*You* want to be the one who stands out by being the one who doesn't want to stand out. The one who bought the book for innocent reasons."

"But I didn't buy the book-"

"Irrelevant. Admit defeat Ruth. The verdict is in. Case dismissed."

His thoughts have taken him even further away from me than normal, and his attempt to close the gap between us by pulling me nearer feels clumsy. His tongue passes through my lips but his words still linger upon it and fill my mouth with a bad taste. I pull away from him as casually as I can.

"What's the matter? Are you sulking?"

"No. It's just that…'

"What?"

I need to tell him the real story about the book; that it is based on me. Whether he believes me or not, I need him to know the reason I introduced him to the subject. And what's more, he might be able to represent me when I take Walden to court.

I take a deep breath, and start to talk. His face contorts into a series of frowns.

"That's ridiculous, why would the book be about you?"

"I don't know. I just know that it is."

"Oh come on… you expect me to believe your book club sent you a loyalty gift and you just so happen to be the main character in it?"

"I know it sounds far-fetched, but–"

"Far-fetched? It's mental, Ruth. And who even buys books from a book club these days anyway?"

"I do."

"Well you shouldn't. Get a bloody Kindle."

"I like books I can hold. Physical books."

"You don't seem to like this one very much. And neither do I. We should be shagging by now. Not talking about literary fantasies."

He's staring at me with his head cocked to the side, as if we've reached the end of the discussion. But we haven't. Because I don't want another man running round with the wrong impression of me.

"It's not a fantasy, it's there. Black on white."

"Show me. Where's the book?"

Knowing he's not my ally in this, the thought of sharing Walden's words is frightening.

"We don't have to read it. We can just go upstairs."

"Back pedalling now, are you? If you think you're featured in some two-penny give-away book, I want to read all about it. So go on, where is it?"

I stand to get it, wishing I hadn't brought it up at all.

"I should warn you that he doesn't paint a very favourable picture of me."

Before I can start to read, Paul snatches the book out of my hands. I can't gauge from his expression what he's thinking, but it doesn't matter, because he doesn't keep me waiting for long.

"I don't get it. What makes you think this is you?"

"The physical description. Like I said."

"You mean this stuff about the dress?"

"And the scar and the shoulder length red hair."

As I utter them, the words sound thinner than the hair they describe. I can't meet his eye, but I don't need to in order to know he is re-evaluating me as a narcissistic fantasist. Yet, neither can I sit here and fail to defend myself.

"And a little bit further on there's a bit about a bag which is just like mine, and the fact that the woman waits for everyone else to get off the train before she does, which is exactly what I do too."

"Where?"

"When we get to London."

"No. I mean, where in the book?"

I try to retrieve it from him to cover up my embarrassment for thinking he was engaging with me, but he holds it tight, so I have to point to the relevant passage in his hands. He starts to read out loud, smirking at me when he reaches the part about the bag and Davina's disembarkation habits. He doesn't stop there either, but continues reading, and, as he does, I pick up on a detail that had so far escaped me.

"Wait a second."

Paul keeps going until the end of the sentence.

"Can you read that bit again?"

"Which bit?"

"The bit you just read."

He looks at me with impatience and holds the book out of my reach.

"Please?"

"Fine. But you're being really strange tonight.

And twice she was overcome with the certainty that this man, whoever he was, would look magnificent on her arm.

"I meant the next sentence."

The day after the concert, Davina was preparing for a visit from her married Thursday night lover when the telephone rang.

I'm looking at him, but he hasn't registered my alarm.

"I've had enough of playing book clubs. Can we go upstairs now?"

"Weren't you listening?"

"Enough to know that you have a vivid imagination," he pulls me closer again, "and that you are more of a paranoid neurotic than a narcissistic fantasist."

There is a teasing undertone to his voice, but I'm not in the mood for smiling.

"It says Davina has a lover on Thursday nights."

"So?"

"So? So do I."

"Ruth, this is getting tedious."

"But it's Thursday. You are my Thursday night lover. Don't you get it?"

"Are you saying you think this is about us?"

"It adds up."

He starts to laugh.

"To nothing!"

"But it's all true. You come here every Thursday. As my lover."

"Oh, I get it. This is about me not spending enough time with you, isn't it?"

"No."

I detect the note of protest in that one syllable, but somewhere in the distance I also register that he might be right. This, however, is not the time to discuss the flimsy foundation of our relationship. Not when there is even the slightest possibility that Mr Walden has been watching us, because that would mean he knows where I live and, if he knows that, then he didn't only see me on the train, but must have followed me home. And if he followed me home, what else does he know? But then again... of course... why didn't I think of that sooner?

"Is it you?"

"What?"

"Are you the writer?"

"Me?"

"Yes. That would explain–"

He looks genuinely puzzled.

"I'm a solicitor who works sixty hours a week. I have a... I have a busy life. Why the hell would I want to assume a pseudonym to write a book about you, correction, about you and me?" Spelled out like that, it doesn't sound very plausible.

"I just thought..."

"And to completely burst your bubble, it says 'married Thursday night lover.'"

"But–"

"No buts Ruth. You're running away with yourself. The book is not about you. What it describes is totally generic. It's a fact that about 60 percent of all married men have affairs. I could name a dozen from my office alone, and almost all of them have a 'sporting fixture' once a week. Thursday's as good a night as any."

I sink into him, willing myself to buy his theory and forget my own.

"So… are you going to let us do what Thursday night lovers do?"

I'm not really in the mood, so I don't immediately respond.

"Bloody hell Ruth, if I'd known you were going to be such a bundle of fun tonight, I'd have invited my friends along as well."

I sincerely doubt that, since I've never met a single one of them.

"Would you?"

"You know what your trouble is, Ruth? You spend too much time on your own. You should go out more. Less brooding, more socialising. Go on a couple of dates."

"Why would I want to go out on dates when I've got you?"

"We're just having fun together. We agreed on that."

I didn't. I look at him to see if he's joking, but his face is serious.

"Oh come on, don't give me that look. It's my philosophy."

It is the first time I've heard him talk about this particular philosophy, and when he takes my hand to lead me upstairs a few minutes later, I don't feel like going with him. But since he is the only man I have, I ignore my instincts and tramp up behind him.

- 9 -

He had been waiting two weeks and six days for her to start reading the book he dropped through her letterbox, and which he hopes will bind them more tightly than it is bound itself. He was glad, when he saw her put it into her bag two mornings ago, to see that he need wait no more, and that she had finally embarked on the journey he devised for her.

He is not pleased, however, that she has invited Thor to join her on her travels through his words, and even less so that she has allowed him to read those words aloud to her. He is concerned that the truth about Thor's marital status will be twisted when delivered through his lying lips. He does not like lies any more than he likes betrayal, which he does not like one iota.

He had hoped she would instantly understand from the book that the man sitting snugly by her side is already taken, but wonders now if he was too subtle. That being a possibility, and Thor having definitely outstayed his welcome in her life, he turns his mind to the different ways he has so far considered removing him from the picture. He silently warns Thor that he might meet with one or other fate if he does not begin to take seriously the institution of married life, *Long-term commitment to spoil one before mixing five hundred I feel. (7, 4)*, and to remember the vows, *All promises as Robert the old pop idol makes painful cries (4)* he took at his wedding, *Joining together in a Berlin suburb (7)*.

He would like to reassure her that she does not need Thor. He would like to tell her, too, that she will have no need for any Thursday night lovers once she has read the book and her life has changed course to integrate him at its core. He would like to reassure her that she will be spared the pains of seeking a groom, *Small jumper in genetically modified state makes for a stable person (5)*, and that he will never expect her to walk down the aisle dressed in a frilly wedding dress, *Make Waldo bring a special dress (6, 4)*.

He does not believe she will linger over Thor's sudden but necessary departure, because her mind will be preoccupied with the tasks ahead of her; planning the funeral and their future thereafter.

- 10 -

It is three forty-five. Paul has been gone for hours. Following his declaration that I am just a passing phase, I didn't dare ask him to stay. But without him I can't sleep. I keep going over the conversation we had about Walden's book. I know he is probably right about the number of men ostensibly breaking a sweat at the squash club while actually making merry with their mistresses, but I'm also sure I'm right about my role as Davina. Since the publisher is unable or unwilling to help, the next place to turn has to be the book club. I look for their contact details in the last brochure they sent me. I find a postal and email address, but no telephone number or website.

To: RMorton@BaldNoMore.co.uk
From: Info@BicycleBooks.co.uk
Subject: The Ruthlessness of One Man by Mr Walden

Dear Sir or Madam,

I am writing to thank you for the copy of Mr Walden's 'The Ruthlessness of One Man' you sent me as a loyalty gift last month. It might surprise you to learn that I seem to be the stranger on whom the writer modelled his protagonist.

Since making the discovery I've been trying to contact the author, but so far to no avail. Dragonfly Press, which is cited in the book as his publisher, tell me they have neither Mr Walden nor the title on their list. All very confusing.

That is why I'm approaching you for help. As a distributor of 'The Ruthlessness of One Man', I feel confident that you must know which Dragonfly Press published it and how I might reach them. I'd be grateful if you could forward me that information as quickly as possible.

I realize this is probably an unusual request, but it is crucial that I make contact with the author. I thank you in advance for your time and help, and look forward to hearing from you ASAP.

Thanks and best wishes
Ruth Morton

I send the mail and go to the only other place I think might be of help in my search for the elusive author: my sofa. *The Ruthlessness of One Man* is still lying on the arm where Paul left it when he decided he would rather have the real over the fictionalized me a few hours ago. However much I want to leave my alter-ego to her own fate, I can't.

She is still sitting outside the British Library, absurdly in awe of this "gentleman" who refuses to reveal his name, and is absurdly in awe of himself. He has just finished telling her he has what it takes to become a conductor of world renown, but that his chances have been thwarted by other people who refuse to give him the breaks he deserves.

> *"I am enjoying sitting here talking to you, Davina."*
> *"So am I."*
> *"You belong in my life."*
> *"Really?"*
> *"Yes. Does it please you to hear that?"*
> *"Yes."*
> *"Good. It pleases me to please you. Now, I'm afraid I must be going, but I would like to leave you with this thought: If perfect strangers strangers be, then strange it seems how perfectly their paths crossed once in such a way, that twice should come another day."*
>
> *With that, Dear Reader, the gentleman leaned over and kissed Davina softly on the head. Had it not been for the fact that he then stood to leave, she would have collapsed into his protective arms. Instead she watched him walk towards the road. He had almost reached it by the time she caught up with him again.*
>
> *"Won't you give me a name to call you until I know you well enough to know your real name?"*
>
> *He stopped, took a step back towards her, and with a tip of his hat, he said: "Very well. For the time being, you may call me Mr Walden. Mr Tod Walden."*

I gasp as I throw the book on the floor. I kick it away and it hits the far wall with enough force to crumple the pages. My whole body is screaming danger, and I am acutely aware of a sense that there is more to *The Ruthlessness of One Man* and my role in it than I have previously thought.

Fragments of comprehension are floating around one another and around me. There are my clothes, my hair, my behaviour, my Thursday evening lover, a man who saw me on a train, another who wants me to plan a funeral with him, and yet another who happens to have the same name as the author of the work in which he appears. Exactly who is who, and who signifies what, I have no idea. And for long minutes I just sit and stare at the book lying discarded and toxic against the skirting board on the other side of the room. I don't want to touch it again. Or even look at it.

I get up.

I can't think straight.

My mind is darting in all directions, colliding with itself at every turn.

I sit down.

I'm up again, pacing for clarity, but there is none to be had.

The room is too small for my thoughts.

I go into the kitchen and put on the kettle.

I should phone someone. The police, perhaps? But what could they do?

Paul? No.

I go back to the living room. The book is still splayed against the wall like a huge spider staring at me with silence and stealth. I'm on my own with Tod Walden. And if I want to be rid of him, I can't cower. Watching the paperback from the corner of my eye, I type his name into my computer. Apart from a couple of references in German, I find one listing for a South African dentist and a number of etymological entries which claim Tod to mean 'fox' or 'wily'.

Is the real Mr Walden wily? Does he really know about Paul? Has he followed me home? The seed of that thought, planted when my lover read aloud to me, has already matured and is suggesting he might have broken into my house, been in this very room. My blood floods with the memory of the recent and unsettling discovery of my kitchen knife somewhere I know I didn't leave it. I had been looking all over the kitchen for it for two days when it suddenly turned up on the bathroom windowsill. I convinced myself that I must have been using it when I went upstairs to get something, and put it down to wash my hands. But now, in these twilight hours, I'm willing to believe that whoever wrote *The Ruthlessness of One Man* also moved the knife.

I re-boil the boiled kettle.

I check my mail again.

It's 5.45. There will be no mail for hours to come.

I make tea.

I add sugar for the first time in years.

I need strength.

My only lead is the book club and I have to get a reply from them, even if it means going all the way to Scarborough myself.

- 11 -

James Hunter had always dreamed of being an investigative journalist. Throughout his teenage years, he had
nurtured a mental image of himself in a trench coat, wired
up and only ever two steps away from breaking the news
which would bring the nation to its knees and him into contact with the royal sword. His lunchtimes would be spent in
pubs entertaining racy women with anecdotes of his most
adventurous of adventures. While he had managed to pull
off a diluted version of his perfect midday break, the closest James ever came to living his reporter dream was at
night, when his eyes flickered excitedly beneath their lids.

He was just twenty years old when he met Suzie the
floozy, as he had later learned was her nickname. Within a
matter of hours her body was making space for an unwanted member of the next generation and soon thereafter
James was forced to acknowledge that he had made his bed
in a bed on the coast of North Yorkshire. As he lay in it
during the long years to come, he would listen to the waves
crashing against the South Bay promenade and wish, above
all things, that they had carried him away to Fleet Street
before his lust had determined his fate.

Two years later another baby came along and, although
James may have been given to dreaming and impulsive-
ness, he was not without a sense of responsibility, and did
his best by Suzie and the kids. In the early years he spent
the tourist season waiting tables at the cliff top Grand Hotel
or the restaurant at the Spa Theatre, earning his wage and a
bit on top in tips. He put by what he could, because however much work Scarborough had to offer in the summer,

when winter rolled around, the shutters along the sea front rattled to a close, locking away the jobs inside.

When, in their fourth summer together, Suzie left him for a man with a villa in southern Spain, James was only partly broken. He would miss his children, but was not entirely averse to the idea of a more carefree existence. So, after waving them off at the airport with kisses and promises of an imminent visit, he packed his own bags and boarded a train for Manchester: the London of the north, as he saw it.

He strutted the city streets, embracing what he liked to refer to as his belated youth. He wore sunglasses, rented a bed-sit, and found work cleaning the offices of the local gazette – a job he momentarily allowed himself to believe was a springboard to his journalistic aspirations. He revelled in the city's pubs and slept with the city's women but, as the nights began to draw in, he was overcome with a choking feeling of homesickness.

He longed to breathe the air of Scarborough's plaintive winter skies. He found himself aching with the need to do something more with his life than clean; something that would keep both the wolves and himself from his drab front door.

When he went back to Scarborough for Christmas that year, it was for good. And it was with a plan. If his own words were not destined to earn him a place in the annals of great journalism, if he was not to be immortalised on paper, then he could at least spend his days among those who had.

He convinced the bank to grant him a modest loan, rented a tiny garret on one of the narrow lanes overlooking the sea, contacted publishers, printers, and the postal service, and officially registered his company under the name of Bicycle Book Club. So called because from now on in, he would be peddling books all over the country. A rather clever name, he thought.

In the eight years since beginning his mail order business, James had not exactly become rich, but he made ends meet. And although he periodically still saw himself scribbling shorthand in the name of serving his country, there was something he quite liked about running 'Bicycle' as he called it for short. It gave him time to himself. Anyone who wanted to disturb him had to climb three flights of stairs to do so, and most people he knew preferred to meet him in the comfort of the local pub than struggle to such an altitude.

He had a phone but it rarely rung, not least because he believed a mail order company should be just that and had never given his customers his number for fear they might start calling him to chat about books.

He would, he told himself, get around to setting up a website and digitizing his entire company one of these days, but so far, he had not received enough complaints about his analogue system to necessitate the move away from paper order forms, stamps and envelopes. He did have an email address, so that anyone who really wanted to get in touch with him at great speed could do so. But as the bulk of his customers failed to realise they were living in a digital age, he was not often the recipient of anything besides advertising circulars.

It had come as a bit of a surprise, therefore, when James opened his mailbox on Friday morning to read an email from one of his customers thanking him for a book he had allegedly sent her as loyalty gift. She said it would no doubt be of interest to the Bicycle Book Club to know that, ironically enough, the book in question had been written about her. She was keen to get in touch with the author but having failed to do so, insisted it was up to James to tell her everything he knew about both publisher and author.

That would be easy, he had thought on reading the mail. He could tell her absolutely nothing because he had no idea what she was talking about. Not only had he never heard of Mr Walden, he had most certainly never felt a need to thank anyone for their loyalty. The woman must have been mistaken. Or mad. Either way, James had not considered it his job to reply to the mail and, in that spirit, had filed it under 'trash'. He thought nothing more of it until Friday afternoon when he was yanked out of a daydream by the wholly unfamiliar sound of the door to his office being opened by someone other than himself.

Even if he had had time to consider who the unexpected visitor might be, his imagination would not have supplied him with the captivating sight which stood before him. She wore a dark beret pulled down over shoulder-length red hair, a navy blue coat, and a look of awkward shyness.

"Is this the Bicycle Book Club?" she asked him with a soft Scottish lilt that made him want to know more about her.

"It certainly is. Come in. How can I help you?"

"My name is Ruth Morton. I wrote you a mail about a book you sent me."

"Is that so?" James asked, playing for time enough to place her name.

"It was a loyalty gift."

That was all he needed.

"Now there's a coincidence, I was planning to reply to you today."

James heard the uneven note in his voice and felt his eyes cast about the room, even though he knew they would prefer to be looking at hers. There was something about the woman in front of him, something far more enchanting than his mental image of the Ruth Morton he had so casually signed off as a lunatic.

- 1 2 -

Her chores finished in good time, Morna had time to sit down with a cup of tea and the newspapers. Back in the days when her daughter had lived with her she had been happy to read the Scottish broadsheet and forget that England even existed but, as time had moved on without bringing Ruth back home, she had switched her allegiance to a London paper. These days she was far less interested in the wrangling that went on in Westminster than she had been during the years she had lived within its limits, but she couldn't deny she liked to touch the pages that had been printed in the city where her daughter worked, and was happy to imagine a truck full of newsprint driving past Ruth, or Ruth reading the same publication, or frequenting the local places to which it made reference. All this made her feel closer to the little girl she had once rocked to sleep in time to the winter waves. Besides, she preferred the crosswords in her new paper.

She liked a good cryptic puzzle, particularly the themed ones that appeared twice a week. She enjoyed fishing about within the clues to find out what the day's topic was going to be. It sometimes took her a while to work it out, but once she had, the puzzle was hers. *Spry Leo deranged by affliction (7)*. Affliction equals illness of some kind... spry leo... Anagrams were second nature to her. Writing in her obligatory pencil, she scribbled down 'leprosy'. *Nothing to link gas and linear measures in this mercurial device (11)*. She wasn't sure about that and would have to come back to it. *Les, our cubist becomes all consuming (12).* Les, our cubist becomes must indicate another anagram... Yes... tuberculosis. And she had it. The theme was illness. *Public land which is rarely warm. It's viral! (6,4)* Common cold. And so it went on.

She knew it didn't change her life to complete two dozen clues on the back of a newspaper, but it gave her a sense of satisfaction she hadn't derived from many things in life. She often found herself wishing that Ruth were there to do the crosswords with her, to do with her all the things she hadn't suggested in the long years they'd shared her now lonely home.

Morna wondered again where she had gone wrong, and if her daughter might have become more of a companion if she'd been less protective and less afraid of the person she might become. Right now, she knew very little of that person and, as long as Ruth insisted on living so far away and coming home so seldom, Morna feared it would stay that way, and that she would go to the grave knowing as little of her child as her child did of her.

- 13 -

It's hard to imagine the crisp, clean books I receive in the post from the building I'm now standing outside. It is a far cry from any of the images my unreliable mind had sketched out for me, and Paul's talk of reading books electronically suddenly seems appealing. There are wires poking out of the bell and the intercom system clearly doesn't work. There's no plaque to suggest the book club is housed inside these scruffy red brick walls, and were it not for the fact that I've travelled two hundred miles to get here, I'd turn round and go home.

As it is, I carefully push the door open with my foot, holding it with my shoulder as I slide inside. I'm immediately hit with smells of urine and fried fat. I walk up the first few steps, not touching the banister, which is encrusted with what looks like dried phlegm. I think my loyalty may have been rewarded for the first and last time.

I go up two flights of stairs, past doors of different colours, reminding myself that I'm here for a reason. As I round the last bend in the stairwell, I see a print out of a penny-farthing, under which are the works Bicycle Book Club. I'm so relieved to see it that I don't care about the state of the door in which one of the frosted glass panels has been replaced by a piece of dirty chipboard. There's no bell, so I offer a cursory knock and walk inside.

In the centre of the room, surrounded by boxes, is a single desk and swivel chair in which a man is sitting, staring at me. His red hair is scruffy and he has the look of someone who has neither slept nor shaved for a couple of days.

He looks at me shiftily, as if I've caught him with his pants down.

"Is this the Bicycle Book Club?"

"It certainly is. Come in. How can I help you?"

He has a Yorkshire accent. The kind I've heard on television series set on the moors. Not all his words come out fully formed, but there's something warm about them none-theless.

"My name is Ruth Morton. I wrote you a mail about a book you sent me."

"Is that so?"

"It was a loyalty gift."

"Now there's a coincidence… I was planning to reply to you today."

I'm not convinced.

"I wasn't sure. And since I hadn't heard back, and it's very important to me, I thought I'd come and see you in person."

He leans forward in his chair, elbows on his desk, and hands acting as a support for his bristly chin. He can't hold my eye, which gives me a moment to steal a look at the part of the room facing me. The walls, in which there are two tiny windows offering a framed view of the sea, are lined with shelves, themselves loaded with books.

The man springs to his feet. He's tall and looks even more dishevelled upright than he did sitting. His thick jumper, which does little to conceal his slight frame, is frayed at the cuffs. He puts his hand out to shake mine.

"I'm James Hunter. Founder and Managing Director of the Bicycle Book Club."

He pauses, then points to the swivel chair at his desk.

"Please sit down. I don't have another chair. Being a mail order company, I don't get many visitors."

I walk towards the chair.

"Can I take your coat?" He closes the flaps on a large cardboard box and starts pulling it towards the chair, from which I now have a different view of the room.

"No thank you."

"Or make you a cup of tea?"

Next to the door is an old sink, brimming with cups and dirty water.

"I'm fine, thanks. I had a drink on the train."

He positions his box rather too close to my chair and sits.

"That's good, because I'm actually clean out of tea. I'd have had to go and ask old Mrs Beaumont downstairs, and she can be a bit testy if you interrupt her daytime telly."

The book club man claps his hands and rubs them enthusiastically.

"Right then, down to business." He gets up again. "Sorry, if I could just..."

His shoulder is level with my chest, which is alive to a sense of danger induced by his proximity. I instinctively pull away from whatever it is that is going to happen next.

"...just get at my computer for a moment, I can pull up your mail."

From the corner of my eye, I watch as he opens his mailbox. He goes straight to trash.

"Let me see... oh yes, here it is," there's no embarrassment in his voice, "...so you want to know who published *The Ruthlessness of One Man*...?"

"Yes please."

He sits back down and looks in my direction, but not in my eye.

"Tricky."

"Sorry?"

"It's tricky. What I mean is there must have been some kind of mix-up because I never sent you a book called *The Ruthlessness of One Man*. And I don't have a loyalty scheme. I might get one going in the future, although that's not really what I'm about."

Reams of questions are forming in my mind, but not one escapes my lips. I look at him, waiting for him to tell me he's just joking. But he doesn't.

"I'll confess, I've never actually heard of..." he looks at my mail for reference, "...Mr Walden. Does he not have a first name?"

"I don't know. Maybe Tod."

"Is he a new writer? That could explain it, because I've heard of most writers, you know. The old, the young, the good, the bad, and the dead. Not the self-published, mind you. There are so many of them about these days I can't keep up. I swear they'll run me out of town eventually."

"I'm sorry, Mr Hunter, I don't understand."

"Call me James. We don't stand on ceremony in Scarborough."

I decide to call him nothing, but take Walden's book out of my bag and put it down on the desk.

"I received this book with this compliment slip through the post about three weeks ago."

Thankfully, I tucked the slip in question between the pages of the book, so I have it with me. It bears the same image of a penny-farthing as the sign next to the door, and is printed with the words A LOYALTY GIFT FROM THE BICYCLE BOOK CLUB. I hold it up for him to read, embracing a glimmer of hope that it will jog his memory. He takes it from me, reads it and turns it over. The back is blank. He raises an eyebrow.

"All very mysterious."

A light has gone on in his eyes. One has gone out inside me.

"Very mysterious indeed...' He leans in towards me as if to share a secret, "I don't have any of these slips. Never have had."

"But this... It says it's from you."

"I can see that. But it's not."

It barely seems possible.

"I don't understand."

"Me neither. But I can assure you I didn't send you this."

If what he says is true, Walden has deliberately led me up another wrong path, and in order to do that, he would need to know that I'm a member of this club. And nobody knows that. Nobody that is, except me, Paul – as of yesterday - and the man sitting opposite me. With that thought foremost in my mind, James Hunter no longer only looks scruffy, but scary. The plausibility of his being Walden is suddenly very real. Too real for me to stay here.

All I see of him as I grab my bag and make a run for it are his feet. I notice he's wearing trainers, and I memorise the two white lines that cut through their vivid shade of blue, as a witness might make a mental note of a registration plate. I pound down the stairs, straining to hear the sound of his footfalls behind my own.

Before I know it, I am back outside. Although I have no idea where I am or where I'm going, my instincts tell me to keep moving towards the promenade. Fast. I can hear the sea growling to the wind that whips it, but I can't see it, and am bound to the lie of the streets to get there. I take a left, then a right and another right. I'm in a maze of lanes that feel like they want to trap me. Gulls circle overhead screaming loudly, as if to show the world where I am.

Out of nowhere, the streets of my labyrinth widen, and another left yields a road that runs straight downhill, affording me a glimpse of the great, grey sea. I hurry on, anxious to be closer to the water and further from the building I have left somewhere behind.

There are people on the promenade, but none of them are wearing the blue trainers I'm expecting to see. My eyes on constant alert, I sit on the low wall and catch my breath, listening to the waves crash behind me. They spray my head with salty spit and, for a moment, I am distracted enough by the elements to feel excited by the scene. I imagine myself being carried off on a freak crest to a far away place where there is no writer called Mr Walden. But as soon as I allow his name to pass though my mind, I'm back in the here and now, and he's dragging me up the hill to the poky room filled with books, clichés and unsettling possibilities.

I replay the scene with the book club man. Our sitting together, his retrieving my mail from his trash folder, his telling me he had never heard of Walden or his work, and his insistence that he did not write the compliments slip.

"Oh shit, the compliments slip! Oh no. No, no, no..." I don't need to look through my bag to know it does not contain the book.

I'm so stupid.

I'm going to have to go back and get it.

I don't want to.

I have to. If James Hunter is the author, which right now I feel he might be, then the fact that he lied to me means he must be hiding something. I tell myself I don't want to know what that something is, but I know I'm lying. The truth is that I'm afraid to return to his office alone. But what choice do I have when besides the book itself, the man who says he didn't sent it to me is the only lead I have.

I get to my feet and start to walk in the vague direction from which I came. But then I have another idea. It seems as logical as it does illogical. I could try to buy another copy.

*

The bookshop is well stocked but there is no Walden between Wagner and Walker.

"Can I help you?" A shop assistant is smiling at me.

"I'm looking for a book by a man called Mr Walden. It's called *The Ruthlessness of One Man*.

"If you come with me, we can have a look in the computer."

The assistant's words are delivered with the same accent I encountered in James Hunter's office and I follow them to a desk at the other side of the shop. She glides behind it with a grace that seems out of step with the simplicity of her voice.

"Is it a work of fiction?"

"I think so."

"So… it was Mr Wa…?"

"Walden."

"Do you have a first name?"

I contemplate telling her to look under Tod, but make a snap decision against it.

"No."

"Okay, just Walden then. And the title was *The Ruthlessness...*"

Her emphasis on the first syllable makes me uneasy. But I push the thought away.

"The Ruthlessness of One Man."

She angles the computer screen so that we can both see it.

"I've got a Peter Walden and a George Walden, but no Mr. Could he have either of those first names?"

"Maybe."

"Let's see... Well, neither of them have written anything called *The Ruthlessness of One Man*, so let's try the title..."

She types the words into her computer and a long list appears on the screen.

"Let's have a look...'

She scrolls down, murmuring.

"*Ruthless Boss*, *The Rules of Ruthlessness*, *Ruthlessness in Public Life?*"

She looks at me hopefully. I shake my head.

The entries on her computer screen have become a blur, and she is searching on her own now. I'm too busy trying to make sense of what I'm pretty certain is going to be another dead end.

It is.

"I'm sorry, but I can't find a listing. Do you have any other information?"

Only that it is about me and that both the publisher and the distributor claim never to have heard of it. But I can't tell her that. I shake my head.

"Might it be self-published? Because if it is, it wouldn't necessarily show up on my system."

I have no idea how it was published, but I thank her for her help and, not quite trusting my legs, set out across the carpeted floor to the exit. I'm aware of the coldness of the air into which I step, but I don't feel it. I sit on a bench feeling as feeble as the old woman beside me appears to be.

We sit side-by-side for many minutes. It is she and I versus the steady stream of shoppers who pass us in all directions. Although we neither speak nor even exchange a smile, I find some comfort in the proximity of her hunched back. I look over at her and try to catch her eye, but she doesn't need me as much as I suddenly feel I need her. She is oblivious to my existence. A moment later she stands. Two more after that, she has shuffled away, leaving me alone with the realisation that, even if Walden had self-published, it would not explain why his book was delivered to me from the Bicycle Book Club. Knowing I now have no choice but to go back there is a reality that weighs heavy in the gathering dusk of this unfamiliar town.

- 14 -

He has not seen her all day today and that is not good. He saw Thor leave around 11.30 and watched her return to the sofa where they had engaged in their pre-fornication ceremony, and drink the wine he considers inappropriately cheap for a woman of her calibre.

He hoped to see her resume reading the book which lay discarded on the table in front of her, and was disappointed that it remained untouched as she drank what was left in her glass, turned off the living room light, and went upstairs. A moment later she appeared in her bedroom, and he was surprised to see her open the curtains that had veiled her sexual escapades, and look out across the street, directly into the room where he sat in the arms of darkness, confident that she could see nothing of him.

He watched her until she finally retreated and turned out her light. Only then did he set his alarm to rise thirty minutes before her usual time of waking. But, when he looked out of his window this morning, it was to the unusual sight of both her bedroom and living room curtains half-drawn, and her nowhere to be seen.

He initially assumed her to be in one of the rooms at the back of the house, and patiently waited for her to appear. When, after thirty-three minutes, she failed to do so, he reassured himself that she had, more than likely, gone to the corner shop, and looked towards the end of the road down which he expected to see her amble at any minute. But she did not, and by the time an hour had passed, he had accepted the fact that in her world, open curtains mean she is out, closed curtains mean she is asleep, and half-open, half-closed mean she has gone away.

He scans what he can of her home for an indication as to her whereabouts. The wine glasses and bottle are where she left them last night. So is the cardigan Thor helped her out of before leading her upstairs. The book, however, is gone from the coffee table, and he cannot see it anywhere else either. He assumes, therefore, that wherever she is, his story is with her, which is where it must be if she is to understand her destiny, *Some French have very small following, but make a lot (7)* and see the truth, *Driving aid and famous Moabite are incontestable (5)*.

He does not like it when she goes away, and is surprised not to have noticed any signs of her imminent departure. Her suitcase is still in its place on top of the cupboard in her bedroom, and he did not witness the ritual laying out of clothes that generally precede her holidays. He assumes therefore that wherever she has gone, she has not gone for long. And that fact could well mean she has understood his message to her about Thor's marital status, and has decided not to leave everything to the hand of fate, *Unexpected outcome is put off after cards are dealt then consumed (4,2,4)*. It is, therefore, possible that she has broken it off with him, and has retreated to lick her wounds. Or maybe she is planning to break up and has gone somewhere to gather strength ahead of the event.

Although he does not like to think of her wasting precious emotion on a man with neither heart nor conscience, he decides to do whatever he can to make what he assumes will be her swift return a pleasant one.

He is excited at the thought and knows what must do next. He hurries to the florist, where he buys eight pink and one white rose. He puts the flowers beneath his overcoat and walks up her path. He knocks at the door, which is protected from view by her unruly privet hedge, and stands back, waiting for her not to answer. While she duly obliges, he crosses to the window and absorbs a close-up view of the room and the contents he already knows so well from afar. He can see her cardigan on the arm of the sofa. The sight of it through only one layer of glass sends a shiver of excitement through him. Standing here, he is close to her. But not close enough.

He knocks again for the sake of decorum and, when there is again no response, he carefully and very quietly, slips a key into her lock.

- 1 5 -

It takes me a while to register that the person in the distance is waving at me. I pretend not to see and put my head
down, watching out for the sight of his approaching feet,
my fingers safely entwined in the handkerchief in my
pocket. A few paces later his blue trainers come into view.
I look up to see him beaming at me.

"Hello."

I attempt a smile.

"Fancy meeting you here." He waves a brown envelope
in the air he has just filled with his latest cliché. "Were you
coming back for this?"

I know exactly what he's talking about, but to let him
know that would be to let him believe we are on the same
wavelength. And I don't want us to be on the same anything.

"I don't know. What is it?"

"Your book. Lucky I bumped into you. I was just about
to take it to the post office."

I reach out to take the envelope, but he lifts it above my
grasp.

"It's all very intriguing."

I hold out my hand and he gives me the parcel.

"I'm just off down to the pub, you want to come with
me?"

"I have to be getting home."

"Tonight?"

"Yes."

"It's a long way to go."

How does he know where…?

"What is?"

"Home. Unless you've moved, which, according to my customer records, you haven't. Did my research you see. I know all about you... It's alright, I'm only kidding. All I know is the books you order and where I send them to."

"Oh."

"So, you coming for a drink or what?"

"I don't think –"

"I did a bit of poking around into that book of yours and I found out something that might interest you."

"What?"

"I'll tell you in the pub."

A teasing smile spreads across his face, and something murmurs to me that he can't be the elusive Mr Walden. I whisper back that he could. Anyone could be, especially him.

"I'd rather you just tell me here."

"Don't be daft. It's too damn cold and windy to stand around like this."

*

The pub's packed with drinkers and the sound of early evening banter. As we push our way to the bar, one or two people greet the book club man with shouts of "ey up, Jim." He asks me what I want to drink but before I can answer, he says he bets I'll be having a gin and tonic. I might have done if he hadn't suggested it. I tell him I'd prefer a glass of red wine.

Though I'm a few feet from the bar, I feel uncomfortably beholden to him while he gets the drinks. I hear one woman ask him who his new friend is, and a man warns me to beware of a charm I find hard to believe exists. I assure him I am here on business but can tell from his exaggerated wink that he doesn't believe me. The whole pub, it seems, is staring at me.

The book man walks towards me, holding two glasses, and with a sideways nod indicates to me to follow him. Like a dog dutifully trotting behind its master, I do as I'm told, trying in the process, to ignore the looks my obedience is attracting.

Seated at a table in an adjoining room, he raises his glass to me cheerfully and tells me they only had house red.

"If it's crap I'll get you something else."

I don't want to be left alone again among his people, so I don't care what I drink.

"Right then… where to begin? I've been thinking about this since you came round this afternoon, and I don't mind telling you I'm stumped. Whoever sent you the book obviously wanted you to think it came from my company. Thing is, like I've already told you, it didn't. Which is strange enough as it is, but even stranger given what you said about the publishers reckoning they've never heard of it."

His arms waving about enthusiastically, he speaks as though he's introducing me to something I know nothing about. It might be the animated talk around us, or his air of naivety, but as I look at him gesticulating and listen to him talking, the idea that his hands wrote the book in mine evaporates.

"The really interesting thing is the ISBN number."

"What ISBN number?"

"The one on your book."

"Why?"

"Hold your horses. I'm getting there…"

He's loving this as much as I'm loathing it. He reminds me of a magician, loading everything he says with the promise of something more to come. Although I'm not looking at him, I feel him staring at me, drum roll growing louder as he waits for me to encourage or praise him for what he's about to tell me. I don't give him the satisfaction he's seeking, but that doesn't hold him back. He leans across the table until his face is so close that I have to look into it. And then he lowers his voice, speaking slowly and deliberately.

"The ISBN number on your book has already been allocated… '

His eyes are aglow with the thrill of his words and their meaning, but since I don't know how IBSN numbers are assigned, his excitement is lost on me.

"...and you know what that means?"

I don't.

"...your book doesn't actually exist!"

He slams his hand on the table as he delivers his verdict, causing me to jump and my wine to slop over the rim of my untouched glass. He's leaning back now, staring at me in anticipation of my stunned response. But if I am stunned, it's at the drama of his hypothesis.

"Of course it exists. I have a copy of it right here."

"Correction..." He has leaned forward again and is talking at me with staged control, "I'd say you have it right there."

"What do you mean?"

"I reckon there's only one copy, and *you* have it."

- 16 -

He quietly closes the door behind him and stands in the hallway, breathing in the scent of her home and life. He hasn't been inside her house for more than a week and is glad to be back among her things. He walks to the coats which hang empty on the pegs at the foot of her stairway, and touches them. His fingers linger, like they always do, on the blue one. He shuts his eyes and brings the fabric to his face. It carries the same smell as the house itself, only more concentrated, and it sends a tremor of excitement through him. It won't be much longer before it becomes a part of his daily life.

He knows enough of the people on this street to know that most go to work during the day, but he's still careful to remain behind the half-drawn curtains as he walks into her living room, picks up the vase of flowers, and takes it to the kitchen. He removes the wilted pink roses and changes the water, *Essential to life of revolting peasant and reigning monarch (5)*, which has turned foul. He puts the new stems inside, carefully arranging them so the white one forms the centrepiece. He then wraps the old ones in the paper from the new and puts the parcel by the front door.

He goes back into the living room and picks up the glass to the left of the empty bottle of cheap wine. He knows it was the one from which Thor drank the night before, and is certain she will not want to come home from her trip to find it waiting for her on the coffee table. He takes a large handkerchief from his pocket, wraps the glass in it, and puts it on the ground. With fierce determination, he brings his heel down on top of it as hard as he can. It is crushed in an instant, yet he grinds it for several long moments before picking up the parcel and slipping it into his jacket pocket.

He carries the empty bottle and her glass into the kitchen, where he discards the former and washes the latter, leaving it on the draining board to dry. He cannot help but wipe down her surfaces, which are not quite up to his own standards. Although she is tidy, hygiene is really not her forte. He will point this out to her as soon as the time is right, and will teach her a thing or two about how to use bleach, *Fifty in a sandy place provide germ killer (6)*, soap, *Detectives tail older person to cleaner? (4)*, a scrubbing brush, *Mutated shrub after single wormwood and a Christmas crooner provide a means to shift the dirt (9, 5)* and a mop, *Backward Brit down under has some head of hair! (3)*.

He climbs the stairs to her bedroom. The door is open; invitation enough for him to go inside. Standing next to her bed, he sees it has been made in a careless fashion. A strand of her hair lies on one of the pillows that have not been plumped and the duvet hangs lower on the left than on the right of the mattress. He likes a well-made bed and knows from past visits that she can do better. He attributes this sloppy abandon to her having been angry with Thor and his infidelious ways, and is therefore, on this occasion, willing to remake it for her. But before that can happen, he needs to feel close to her, so he slips off his shoes and slides between the covers.

- 1 7 -

There are three of us at the table now. I can feel Walden's icy presence.

The book club man's statement is dangling between us like a ball on a string.

"Are you all right?"

No I'm not, I want to say. Anything but. Who publishes a single copy of a book?

"Just thinking about what you said."

I take a big gulp of the wine.

"I know it sounds strange, but it's the best explanation I can think of."

"That doesn't mean it's right."

"It doesn't. But I've been over it and over it, and it makes sense. I'm not saying I understand what the bugger is up to, but I can probably work it out. I'm actually pretty good at solving mysteries. I always know who done it in whodunits."

He's talking at me so fast I can't concentrate on what he's saying.

"What's the book actually about?"

"I'm not sure."

"Loosely,"

"I don't know."

"But you've read it."

"Not all of it."

"Seriously?"

He raises his eyebrows and lifts his pint for a long gulp.

"So you came all the way up here without even reading the book?"

"I read some of it."

"Aren't you curious?"

"No."

"Oh, come on…"

"I don't like the book."

"If someone wrote a book about me, I wouldn't put it down, no matter how much I hated it."

We look at each other. Now I'm the one taking a long drink.

"You're not me."

"Yeah, but this Walden, whoever he is, hasn't only written it *about* you, he's written it *for* you."

"You don't know that for sure."

"Wouldn't you say the title is a bit of a giveaway?"

His question chills me before I've even fully registered it. He's given voice to a worry that started forming while Hazel was eating her custard creams at my desk. But it could still be coincidence.

"No I wouldn't."

"Come on, that must be deliberate."

"I don't see why."

"So aren't you going to read the rest of the book?"

"I don't know. Maybe. Maybe I should just forget the whole thing."

He laughs, but I don't join in.

"As if you'll be able to forget it. It's under your skin now. And I bet if you read the book, you'd find all kinds of clues."

"You make it sound like a detective story."

"Maybe it is."

"It isn't."

"How do you know if you haven't even read it?"

"I've read enough to know that."

"I know, we could read it together. Even if you don't want to know what it's all about, I do. Don't forget, my company has been dragged into it as well."

I hadn't thought about it like that, but now that I do, the sense of relief is like slipping into warm water. Perhaps I'm not alone with Walden after all.

"I don't want anyone abusing my company's name... Come on Ruth, you don't mind if I call you Ruth, do you? If we work together, we must stand a greater chance of figuring out what it's all about."

I know he's probably right, and I know I came here for answers. But if what he says about the book being written for me is true, I might rather stay in the dark. He seems immune to my reservation.

"Let's start with the facts. When did you get the book?"

"I don't know exactly, about three weeks ago."

"Was there a postmark on the envelope?"

"I didn't look."

"Do you still have it?"

"The envelope?"

"Yes."

"No."

"And what first made you think you were the character Walden has written about?"

"The physical description. The back of the book says Walden's character is based on a real life commuter."

He opens the first page of the book on the table between us, and begins to read.

"So you have a cream and green flowery dress?"

"Yes."

"I bet you look nice in it."

The blood rushes to my face, which I lower so as not to have to meet his eyes. I would like to be back home where my life is shallow enough for me not to feel out of my depth.

"I should get to the station."

"I don't rate your chances of getting back down south tonight."

"I can still make it."

"But you only just got here."

"I have to go to work."

"Call in sick. We have a mystery to solve."

He's enjoying this a lot more than me.

"And besides, our hotels are world famous."

I shake my head.

"How long until your train leaves?"

I have no idea.

"About an hour."

"Oh well, I suppose we'd better make the most of the time we've got then." He gives me the book, but I don't take it.

"You came here to figure out Walden is. So come on, let's get reading."

I take the book.

"Go to where you left off."

I find the page he wants and look at him. His chin seems more stubbly than it was when I first saw him, and there is a childish excitement in his light brown eyes."

"Found it?"

I nod.

"I'm outside the British Library talking to a man; the same man I meet at a classical concert, a man who happens to be called Tod Walden, and has just made me a present of a book called *The Ruthlessness of One Man*."

He takes it from me and starts to read aloud.

Although Tod Walden appeared to disappear as quickly as he had appeared in Davina's life, he was by no means gone. He had made a profound impression, and she wanted to see him again. You see, Dear Reader, there was something very familiar about him. She knew well enough that she had never seen him before and that, to all intents and purposes, he was a complete stranger, yet at the same time, she felt a profound connection to him. And it was to that connection that she wanted to connect.

"What is he on about?"

"I told you, I have no idea."

"That doesn't even make sense. Is the whole thing like that?"

"Pretty much."

"Oh well, no pain, no gain."

As Davina stood on the pavement outside the library and watched her Mr Walden walk away, she could barely stop herself from running after him and begging him to stay. But despite her upbringing, she had too much decorum to allow such a display of emotion, and therefore simply stood, pining in silence for the man who, although she did not know it, was pining for her in equal measure.

Tod Walden would have liked nothing more than to reach out and touch the young woman who had touched his heart and for whom it was now fervently beating. He would have revelled in the opportunity to run his fingers over her hair, to brush it for her and kiss her head. But he understood the importance of timing, and knew it was not yet right. So he walked steadily away from her, knowing all the while that each step he took was actually bringing them closer together.

"This is creepy. It makes it sound as if I'm attracted to him."

"Older men not your thing?" He's trying not to laugh.

"What's so funny?"

He's commuted his chortle into a cough, but it's fake.

"Nothing."

"Why are you laughing?"

"I'm not. I'm smiling'

He cocks his head slightly and blinks at me with what looks like silent knowledge of something I don't know.

Close enough to begin planning the funeral that had no business waiting forever –

"I don't want to hear any more."

He looks up at me.

"You might think it's funny, but this is about me."

"Is it though? I mean, just because he used your face to write a book, and I'm not saying that's right, because I happen to think it's way off, but that doesn't mean the story is about you. It just means the woman in it, this Davina, has your face."

"I don't want her to have my face. She's awful."

"She does sound a bit needy." He laughs again.

I reach for my coat.

"Don't take it the wrong way. I agree with you that it's a shitty thing to do, I'm just saying there might be no need to take it at face value, if you'll pardon the pun. Unless of course you know some old man who wants you to plan his funeral for him."

"It's not his funeral he wants me to plan."

"Whose is it then?"

"Someone called Shelagh. And before you ask, no, I don't know anyone of that name."

"Anything about her characteristics or physical features that sound familiar?"

"There hasn't been a description of her so far. Just her name."

"There might be more to come."

His eyes are reaching over the table to me.

"I'm sorry I laughed. I didn't mean to. I don't think it's funny. Not at all actually, well except his writing."

I feel myself smile. He smiles back.

"Shall we read on?"

I nod.

Shelagh was not a kind woman, and not the kind of woman who deserved to live a long life. She not quite had her three score years and ten, but that, Dear Reader, was –

"Dear Reader? That's weird."

"What?"

"Hang on, I'll tell you in a minute."

…but that, Dear Reader, was her own fault. She would leave in her wake her daughter Davina, who would take to her role as orphan like a mallard to the village pond. She would take to it so well because it would put her in the same league as her literary heroine, 'Jane Eyre', about whom she read with such frequency from the green bound volume at the side of her bed.

He stops and looks at me as if he has just made a discovery. But it is I who has made one. A coldness attacks me from the inside.

"Okay, this is interesting."

Not interesting. Terrifying.

"You want to know why?"

I can't look at him. I don't want to know anything more than I already do. And I don't want him to know that he just described my favourite book.

"Ruth?"

He is leaning over the table again, staring at me. I drain my glass, shuddering as I swallow its rough contents.

"Do you want to know what I am getting at?"

It could just be a coincidence. There could be lots of people who have a copy of *Jane Eyre* next to their beds. It's a classic. The classic of classics. And besides, I've read that book on the train more than once.

"Okay, wait for it… you know I said the ISBN number on *The Ruthlessness of One Man* is already taken? Well, it's taken by an edition of *Jane Eyre*."

I hear his words, but can't work out their significance, if indeed there is any. Again he is waiting for my response. I lift my glass to my lips. It's empty.

"You know what I think, Ruth?"

I clench my teeth, willing him to do the same with his and keep his words behind them. My thoughts have dragged me elsewhere, to something neither one of us has thought about until now. How did Walden know I am a member of the book club? I am grappling for an answer, but my mind draws blank after blank.

"I think your man, Walden…'

I can't believe it has only just occurred to me, because now it has, it's so obvious. He can only know by knowing where I live. Even seated, I can feel myself losing my balance.

"…seems to know a lot about you."

More than you know he knows. The coldness inside me swells and freezes.

"I don't want to say anything to upset you Ruth, but do you think it's possible you might be being stalked?"

The anxiety that has been growing inside me for the past days has taken over. I can feel my hands trembling on my forehead but all the sights and sounds around me slip out of focus. The fact that I am sitting across from a relative stranger is incidental. Tears tumble out of me and I am powerless to stop them.

"Hey, don't cry."

I can't see him now.

"Have some of your wine. Shit. It's empty. Shall I get you another?"

I feel him get up from his seat and come closer to me. I don't react when he puts an arm around my shoulder. I don't shrink back when he clumsily wipes my face with the cuff of his jumper. I no longer see how frayed it is. I just feel the comfort it offers. I feel his warmth and I want it to protect me. I lean into him, let him share the weight of my anguish. I hear his heart beating against my ear. It sounds solid and reliable. James. Jim. Whoever he is, I need him. He strokes my head as if I were a child. I don't know how long we sit like that before he suggests taking me outside for some fresh air. But when he does, I let him help me into my coat and lead me onto the seafront.

- 18 -

Morna Morton waited at the shore for the ferry. Coming to the port was a gesture she generally reserved for family – such as it was – and friends. On this occasion, however, she was quite happy to make an exception. She only hoped she would not bump into Betty Jenner, or Jenny Better as the anagram fittingly had it, who was familiar with her custom and would be certain to want to know the significance of whoever was due off the boat. But even if Morna told her, she wouldn't understand. She would think her insane. And perhaps she was. She knew what she was doing went a stretch beyond the ordinary, but Ruth's determination to stay away from the place she was born and bred, and the mother who bore and bred her, left Morna desperate enough to resort to measures to match.

If she had been in the habit of anagramming names at the time of her daughter's birth, she might have anticipated that Ruth would cause her pain and chosen a different, safer name. One that might have spelled out a future closer to home.

As it was, Ruth had gone to London with everything she owned and some things, Morna discovered later, she did not. Most notably her old school copy of *Jane Eyre*.

Morna had begged her daughter not to go, not to London at least, and had tried to convince her that she would be happier and safer in one of Scotland's own cities. She had painted the most unflattering picture of the English capital she could, telling Ruth of her own journey south three and a half decades earlier and of her struggle to make a life for herself there. She had described the dangers lying in wait on every street corner in as much detail as she could allow herself, but Ruth had not been deterred. London was her city of choice.

Although eleven years had passed since the day Ruth climbed aboard the ferry Morna was now waiting for, the image of her departure was still as clear as the day it had occurred. Half the island had turned out to wave her off, and by the time Ruth had finished bidding them all farewell, there was no time left for her mother. All she had got was a hurried hug and a quick kiss on the cheek, as if she were going out for the evening.

As the boat moved slowly across the water, the islanders had turned their attention to her. Everyone had been so full of smiles and words of kindness, but Morna knew that by the time she had crept back up the road to her empty house, their kindness would have turned to pity, and their talk to the whether of Ruth's return. So many others before her had gone and so few had come back for anything more than an annual visit.

In the early months of Ruth's absence, Morna had insisted on at least one phone call a week. Although brief, they had served their purpose of allowing her to feel she knew something of her daughter's new life. But as time had move on, the calls had become more infrequent, and the information they imparted more impersonal.

Likewise Ruth's visits home. They occurred once every twelve to eighteen months, lasted for no more than a week, and taught Morna the square sum of nothing about her child, except that she seemed profoundly unhappy. The less her daughter talked about her life and anyone in it, the more Morna worried that there was something to worry about.

With that in mind, she inched closer to the quay where the boat had just come in and watched for her new guest among the passengers trickling off onto dry land. She had no idea what he looked like, but was sure he would stand out among the ramblers, pilgrims, and holidaymakers. When she caught sight of a tall, slim figure of a man in an overcoat, she congratulated herself on her instincts and moved towards him with outstretched hand.

- 19 -

James had not intended to sleep with Ruth. Had, when she accepted his offer of a drink, he allowed himself to dwell upon how the evening might unfold, he would never have seen it extending to their nakedness in Room 539 of Scarborough's Grand Hotel. He wasn't sure who'd made the first move. Was it her, when she'd tearfully told him about the copy of *Jane Eyre* on her bedside table? Was it him, when he'd offered to find her a place to stay for the night? Was it her, when her eyes had silently pleaded with him to stay a little? Or was it him, when he'd poured the wine he'd brought from the pub into the plastic cups from the bathroom? James didn't know. What he did know, however, was that from a certain point onwards he had taken control of the situation.

They had been standing side by side, silently contemplating the blackness of the sea of death below them, when James had felt his old ambition tug at him. For once he did not dismiss it as a long gone dream, but gave in, allowing himself a taste of the man he had wanted to become; the excellent investigative reporter who entertained enigmatic, elegant women such as the quiet red-haired beauty beside him. In that guise, it had been only appropriate that he should take her by the hand and lead her to the bed. Ruth had followed him wordlessly, and although that willingness enthralled him, once they were seated there, he was dwarfed by her quiet silence.

He knew very well she was out of his league and was certain she knew it too. While he'd been dispatching books from a poorly heated room in the town of his birth, she'd inspired someone to write one about her. And although James couldn't be sure, he was quite willing to believe that Walden was a pseudonym for one of Ruth's suitors, of whom he was sure, there must be many.

He had tried to stroke her face, but she had turned away, making him all the more nervous and in need of something profound to say. In the end, he asked her what she liked about *Jane Eyre*. She had just looked at him sadly and, fearing that she might start to cry again, or even ask him to leave, James leaned in to kiss her. Even as it was happening, he was aware of the significance of the moment. James Hunter seducing somebody else's muse. The thrill of the realisation was overwhelming, and before he knew it he and Ruth were lying on the bed where he was unbuttoning her blouse.

- 20 -

All I keep thinking is that I don't know this man on top of me. When the lights were on I had his face, unfamiliar as it is, as a vague point of reference, but in the darkness I have nothing to hint at his identity. His movements, naked skin, and the noises he makes are all so foreign. I touch his back, hoping it might help me to see him, but instead I see Paul. In my mind's eye he's watching me betray him, but he doesn't care. Far from chastising me, he's egging me on, congratulating me for not getting too attached to him.

Paul stays with me until the book club man takes my face in his hands and asks me if I'm all right. His accent brings me back to the hotel room and the bed with the nylon cover which I'm trying to keep from slipping to the floor. It brings me back to him, and to what we are doing, the two of us.

Am I all right?

I nod, not knowing whether he can see and far less whether it's true. How long ago since we sat together in his office, and then in the pub? How long since he led me, his arm around my shoulders, onto the promenade? How long since we walked along the night sand and through the gardens to the cliff top hotel in which we are now consummating our few hours of acquaintance?

He lowers his lips towards mine and I don't resist. I like the freedom of this moment. I feel a surge of excitement and involuntarily pull him closer to me. My mind wanders away from the sex we're having to the morning after. I see myself waking with him beside me and us eating breakfast in bed together before strolling hand-in-hand along the windswept beach below my window, perhaps stopping for a cup of tea at one of the cafes that line it. I might even wear his jumper with the tattered cuffs.

He looks down at me again. I don't know the pattern of his breathing, have no cues to guide me, but it sounds as though we will not be bound together like this for much longer. My body has not kept pace with his and I don't mind that, but I don't want it to end, this closeness. I don't want to be alone. But there is no stopping him now. He lets out a groan of pleasure, gentle compared to the grunting I'm used to, then gradually comes to a halt. He sighs and sags and kisses my forehead before rolling off me, taking our intimacy with him.

We don't look at or speak to each other for what seems like an eternity and with each minute that passes, he on his side of the bed, me on mine, I can feel my senses returning to normal. Uncertainty slips into the space between us. I want him to reach out and touch my face again like he did when he was on top of me, or to hold me like he did in the pub, but he doesn't.

I want to turn on my side, prop myself up on one elbow, and say something, but I don't know what that something might be, so instead I let my hand stray a couple of inches from my side under the bed covers, hoping to encounter something of the flesh which so recently covered my own.

I know he can't be far away, yet he feels so out of reach. A few hours ago, I was irritated by the laughter in his voice, but now all I want is to hear it again. I want him to speak to me, to reassure me that he doesn't regret what we've just done.

"I wonder what time it is."

He turns to look at me.

"I don't know."

"It must be late."

It's a feeble exchange, and miles from the one I want to be having, but at least it has broken the ice. He touches my hand, very lightly, and draws breath to speak. I hold my own hoping he will say he doesn't care how late it is because he's right where he wants to be.

"Yeah, I'd probably better get going."

No. Please don't go. Not now. Not after what we've just done, not after everything you have helped me find out about Walden. You must be able to see that I can't be alone now. You saw me cry. You can't have thought those tears were for nothing. I have to tell him not to leave me by myself in this strange place. I don't want him to go. I have to tell him to stay.

"Okay," I hear my tongue betray me.

"I've got lots of work to catch up on tomorrow. No rest for self-employed hands, and if I stay here all night, I don't imagine either of us will get any sleep…"

His words are force-filled with a gaiety that doesn't match the reality of my being the woman no man wants to spend an entire night with.

"…but I really enjoyed being here with you."

He turns the light on and the room is suddenly filled with the memories of an hour or so ago when we were still dressed and he was my ally. I wish it were still then. I won't feel safe here if he leaves. Walden could be anywhere. He could be in this hotel, waiting in the hallway for me. If he knows enough about me to know which book club I belong to, and which book I have on my bedside table, then he could quite easily have followed me here, could have been sitting behind me on the train, beside us in the pub. He might have overheard our conversation, laughed at our pathetic attempts to figure out his identity and motive.

I want James to stay. Please don't go. Turn and look at me. Please don't leave me here.

"I'm sorry for my emotional outburst earlier."

"No need to be sorry."

He puts his hand on mine as he speaks, and pats it as if I were his grandchild. He has spent all his sympathy. He has seen my body, tried me out, and decided he would rather go home than endure the rest of the night with me in the Grand Hotel of little grandeur. Inside I am shouting at him to wake up to the situation. But outwardly, all I can do is turn away and mentally prepare myself for his departure.

"If you need any help with your book, call me. I'm at your disposal. I wrote my number on the compliments slip, and it's in the envelope with the book."

"Thank you."

He climbs out of the bed. I long to turn round and watch what he's doing, but I won't give him that satisfaction. Instead I listen as he picks up his clothes and goes into the bathroom. He locks the door behind him, but the walls are thin enough for me to make out the sounds of him peeing, flushing the toilet and washing his hands. If it is his hands he is washing. Perhaps it is not. Perhaps he is washing me off his penis. I watch him through closed eyes and a closed door, see him as he smilingly slips back into the tatty jumper. The same one he used to wipe away my tears and the same one he will be wearing when he walks back into the pub not ten minutes from now to buy his friends a round of drinks in honour of his victory, the woman who caused a pathetic public scene at the mere mention of *Jane Eyre*.

- 2 1 -

Morna Morton sat up late with her visitor, who was making a steadier inroad into the bottle of single malt than she'd anticipated. On the whole she didn't like drinkers and was tempted to pass comment but, in the interests of getting things off to a good start, decided to restrict her expression of disapproval to the occasional raised eyebrow. Besides, if even half of what she'd heard about his type over the years were true, alcohol was a part of his job.

He was not entirely what she'd expected. When she'd first read his little piece of text among all the odds and ends on the back pages of her paper, she thought he sounded very professional. There was talk of experience, personal attention, surveillance and confidentiality, but now he was here, almost sprawled on her sofa, downing one whisky after another, she found it hard to equate the description with reality.

He seemed more interested in talking about expenses than anything else. But she had to give him the benefit of the doubt because, although she knew there must be many others like him in London, he appeared to be the only one to advertise his services in her daily paper. In that respect, he was her only option and she was just going to have to make the most of it. The most of him.

He told her he had done a bit of advance sniffing about – for which he would want to be paid - and had found Ruth's house. She thought "found" an exaggeration since she had given him her daughter's address, but was willing to overlook his embellishment in exchange for details about what it looked like. He described it as a "pretty bog-standard semi" on a "pretty bog-standard street" in a "pretty bog-standard suburb", and confirmed that it did not belong to her, but to a man called Mr Malik Ali. Morna would have liked him to take some photographs, but he made it clear he couldn't do that without first checking that she'd be willing to cover the extra costs involved. When she learnt what they would be, she opted to stick to mental images as long as he provided her with all the information he could glean about the life her daughter was leading so resolutely without her.

- 22 -

I am alone.

The feelings of freedom I had while James was here in bed with me have long since evaporated. His absence has filled the room with the presence of a whore and the ghostly whisper of a man who has written about her. I don't want to think about Walden, and to avoid doing so, I haul the memory of James and I, so recent yet already so faded, back to the forefront of my mind, where I try to blow it up to the size of the room. But it keeps shrinking back to Walden, and the thought that he might be standing right outside my door.

Come back James. I forgive you. I don't mind if you used me. I run my hand over the bed, indirectly touching him. I switch on the light to look for any trace of him, but all I see is the envelope containing the book that contains more of me than it ought. I remove the compliments slip I showed him in his office this morning.

Dear Ruth,

It was lovely meeting you today and listening to your story, which has had me guessing all day. Since you and Mr Walden have chosen to include me in this puzzle, which I must admit intrigues me, I've decided to help you in your search for answers. I did a bit of research into the book and found out something I'm certain will be of interest to you. Call me and I'll tell you all about it.

Best wishes
James (Jim)

His 'best wishes' seem so outdated. I stare at his telephone number and can suddenly imagine myself speaking
to him. I'm asking him to come back to the hotel room and,
while I'm asking, he's arriving, getting into bed with me. I
shake the fantasy away and bury myself in the covers in
which his smell mixes with that of fabric softener. I breathe
in what is left of him, following it back to the pub, to talk
of the book that doesn't exist, to the similarities between
me and Davina, to the ISBN on *The Ruthlessness of One
Man*, and to the fear that was briefly tamed by our unexpected sexual encounter.

"Leave me alone Walden, whoever you are."

But he doesn't. He's everywhere here. He's under my
bed, in the grain of the cheap wooden wardrobe, behind the
bathroom door, and in every particle of air in this Scarborough hotel room. I close my eyes and beg sleep to
remove me from this waking nightmare. But there is no
sleep to be had here.

There's a tap at the window.

I hear myself scream.

I'm under the covers. As far as I can get.

My heartbeat is out of control and my legs ache with
dread as I run through the possible explanations for the
noise. Window cleaner. Wind. Perhaps it was the door, not
the window. A hotel employee.

I hear it again and it is definitely the window, not the
wind, not the door. But nobody cleans windows in the dead
of night. The curtains are open but I don't allow my eyes to
stray to the glass. I stay beneath my covers, shaking all
over, sweating. Seagulls screech overhead, laughing at me.
The tapping continues.

"Go away."

My demand comes out in a voice I didn't know I had.

A gull caws, closely, as if in response.

I poke my head out of the covers just as he gives a final
tap before flying away leaving nothing at my window but
the leaden Scarborough sky.

- 2 3 -

He is happy to have her home, *He contains order of merit at his house (4)*, and cannot take his eyes from her living room where she is slumped somewhat inelegantly on the sofa cushions he lovingly plumped on her behalf. He had not imagined she would return so quickly, and is glad to be wrong. He is less happy, however, that she does not appear to be so herself. He had expected her to return full of the joys of a new life without her married lover. It irritates him that she hasn't. He tells himself she is merely tired, that Thor did not make it easy for her to break free of his unlawful clutch.

He watches her rise and wander aimlessly around the room before her attention rests upon the flowers he was kind enough to replace in honour of her homecoming. He sees her pull the white bloom from the vase, *French go south east to hold flowers (4)*, and touch it, petal by petal, her face marked by a look he takes to be one of excitement. He shares in it as she turns to look out of her window towards him.

He blows her a kiss he knows she cannot see, although wishes she could, and appeases himself with the thought that it won't be much longer before she is knocking on his door. For a moment he indulges in thoughts of that future and when he returns to the present, it is to see her on her hands and knees searching for something on the floor.

He watches as she looks on the bookshelves, and under the sofa cushions, her searching becoming gradually more frantic, until she finally leaves the room and goes upstairs to the bedroom, *Where and on what Othello goes back to sleep (7)*.

He admires his own bed making skills, and watches as she looks around the room with a sketchy haste that suggests she does not expect whatever she has lost to reveal itself to her there.

He sees her catch sight of the bed, and can tell she is impressed with his handiwork. From his side of the road, he notes how evenly it hangs to either side, and he sees her note it too. She walks around it and bends over to touch the hem of her bedspread. Again, she looks towards him, and he is seized by a sudden sense that she knows he is there, and that he is responsible for the job well done. He is aware of her appreciation and whispers to her that she is most welcome.

He feels very close to her and, when she dials a number on the telephone which sits on top of *Jane Eyre* beside her bed, he expects his own phone to start ringing. But it does not, so he remains at his telescope by the window, imagining the content and recipient of her call. He believes it is Thor, to whom she is stressing there will be no return to his lair. When he notices her crying, his belief is reaffirmed, and he assumes her tears represent her relief.

He is glad when she hangs up the phone and dries her eyes. He is less glad, though, when he sees her change her clothes and sit at her dressing table, staring into the mirror, *Reflects that daily one is mostly black and white (6)*, in the way she ordinarily reserves for Thursday evenings.

- 24 -

By and large, Magdalena Borkowski followed the hotel rules and did not sit in the chairs or rest on the beds in the seaside rooms she had spent seven days a week cleaning for the past two months. But when, during the last hour of her last shift before her week off, she opened the door to room 539, she was so tired and her feet were hurting so much that she simply had to remove her shoes for a moment. Once they were off, she couldn't resist the temptation to sit down on the edge of the particularly untidy bed and rub them. And once she had done that, she felt a need to stretch her legs out in front of her. So she did.

Although she earned her money cleaning the hotel, she aspired to grander things than the little luxury it offered its visitors. One day, when she had earned enough money to start her own business, she would have them. For the time being, however, she was content enough to sit for a few minutes thinking about what kind of people left a room in such a mess. Passionate ones, she assumed.

As she contemplated who they might have been and where they might have gone, she noticed a book in the bin by the door. She had little time to read but when she did, she preferred Polish romance stories to anything written in English. That being so, she would ordinarily have thrown the book into the refuse sack without so much as peering inside, but for some reason she didn't. Instead she picked it up, settled back on the bed, and began to read. Within a matter of three pages, she had been drawn in and wanted to know whatever the book could tell her about a character called Davina.

And so it was that when she finished making the room look as nice as was possible, she tucked the compliment slip between the pages and slipped the book into her apron pocket. From there, she took it home, and not having time to read it before setting out for the airport the following day, she packed it to read on the plane that would take her home for a whole seven days.

- 25 -

Come on Paul, please hurry up and get here. I have to talk to you, even if you think I'm being paranoid, which I imagine you will. This time though, I don't care. I'm telling you, or at least I will tell you if you ever turn up, that something is not... the bell.

He doesn't look as pleased to see me as I am to see him.

"Shall I take your coat?"

"No need. I won't be staying long."

"Oh, okay... Do you want a drink?"

"No thanks."

"Are you sure? I've got a bottle of wine."

"I'm sure."

His tone invites nothing but a sense of foreboding.

"Just tell me what was so important that you had to drag me here at the weekend. I was playing cricket."

"Won't you at least sit down?"

He looks at the sofa where he usually sits, but opts for an armchair instead.

"So, are you going to tell me or not?"

"I don't know. Maybe I should tell you another day, when you have more time."

"You've got to be kidding. You can't phone me up and cry your bloody eyes out at me to come over here, and then decide it was a false alarm. So come on, what the hell's so urgent?"

He is staring at me with such scepticism that I don't dare tell him.

"I didn't say it was urgent, just alarming."

"Is this a ploy to get me to spend more time with you?"

"Of course not."

"Because it won't work. Not with me. I don't like play-ing games, and I don't like anyone playing them with–"

"I'm not playing games."

"Glad to hear it. So now will you stop being silly and tell me what this is all about? Perhaps we'll even have time to go upstairs afterwards. I've never seen your bedroom in daylight before."

I find myself thinking about James and how he would have reacted had I asked him to come and see me.

"I'll tell you. But will you promise not to be mad with me?"

"I promise."

He's up and walking towards me. I take a deep breath and look at my feet.

"Okay… you remember that book I showed you? The one based on a real person…"

"Yes..." He is sitting next to me now, his hand on the back of my neck.

"I know you think I was being paranoid, but I've found some other things in the book. Things that make me certain it's me."

"Is that what this is all about?"

"It's not only physical characteristics now… the writer, Mr Walden, also knows what my favourite novel is, and where I come from, and my name is in the title, and the ISBN on the book, on my book, the one we were reading, is from a different one, from my favourite novel in fact, and he knows what book club I belong to, which means –'

"Woah… calm down a minute. What exactly are you trying to say?"

"I'm trying to say that I went to Scarborough yesterday to meet the people who sent me the book, except they did-n't, they've never heard of it or of the writer or anything—"

"You went to Scarborough? Shithole. I got food poison-ing there once. One of the worst nights of my life."

I don't know how he managed it, but he has hijacked my story and is now recounting his own, telling me where he ate and stayed on one of "the worst nights of his life." I let him talk, but I'm not listening. I'm recalling my own, more recent memories of the town; its pubs, hotels, and patrons, one of whom has been on my mind a lot today. I'll let Paul have his impressions, and will keep mine to myself. I won't tell him I did as he suggested and went to bed with another man, nor will I share with him the breathtaking dawn sky that slowed my hurried march to the station this morning. I won't try to describe the way the sun hung so low at one end of the promenade that it almost touched the ground, or how its colours stretched across the horizon to the other end where the full moon was bowing out. I won't tell him how comforted I felt by the spectacle, as if nature were reassuring me that, despite all I'd said, heard, and done the night before, I had nothing to worry about. Morning had not only broken, it had broken the spell of fear that had crippled me all night long, and it cradled me on my journey home, talking sense to me, telling me if I really thought I was being stalked, I must collect my evidence and take it to someone who could help me.

But he is not helping.

"I think I'm going to go to the police."

"What the hell for?"

"Because there's enough in the book for me to believe that whoever wrote it is stalking me."

"That's absurd." He laughs.

"I'm not being paranoid, Paul. I know for a fact that someone was in my house while I was away."

"You know what I thought when I first met you? I thought you were down-to-earth and uncomplicated. But now you just sound self-obsessed."

He's staring at me with cold eyes and for a fraction of a second my imagination re-entertains the idea of him as Walden. But the thought is gone before I can grasp it.

"Why the hell would an author be stalking you?"

"I don't know."

"Neither do I. Which is probably because there is no reason."

"I'm telling you Paul, someone was in my house while I was in Scarborough."

He's staring at me, saying nothing.

"Things are different."

"What things?"

"Little things."

"Little things?" He's mocking me, but I know what I saw.

"Yes. Little things. Like the fact that the roses on the table were almost dead when I left and now they're full of life again."

"You're going to have to do better than that."

"I'm serious Paul."

"So am I."

"All right. You see the white rose?"

He nods, but with enough detachment to dilute the argument I have yet to present.

"I didn't buy a white flower. I'm certain I didn't."

"How certain?"

"Completely certain."

"So it faded."

"Flowers don't fade."

"Of course they do."

"Not overnight."

"I'm a solicitor, and I'm not convinced. Tell me how he got it, your stalker? Any smashed windows or other signs of breaking and entering?"

"No."

I know what he's doing, and I know his line of argumentation sounds stronger and more plausible than my own, but I also know he's wrong. I'm no longer in any doubt.

"There was something strange about the glasses too."

"What glasses?"

"The wine glasses we used the last time you were here. I'm sure I didn't wash them before I went away, but when I came back one was washed and on the draining board, and one was missing. How do you explain that?"

"In a court of law there would be any number of suggestions. How about it was late at night, you'd had a couple of glasses of wine, and a good time in bed. When you saw me out, you weren't totally alert, and didn't even notice yourself washing and putting the glasses away, or getting one out again. And who knows how many wine glasses you've got have anyway?"

"I do."

At least I think I do. But perhaps I don't. And perhaps I didn't leave the glasses in the living room. My mind was full of other things.

"I can't prove it one way or the other, but I don't believe you're being stalked. And this wannabe evidence you've given me wouldn't stand up in any court."

"There's one more thing, and I know you'll say it's silly."

"Only if it is."

"The bed was different too. It was made in a way I never make it."

"You're kidding me?"

"No, I'm not. It looked different. Neater. Tidier."

"So you think your stalker breaks into your home, washes your glasses, and makes your bed for you?"

"When you say it like that it sounds ridiculous but–"

"I'm sorry to have to break it to you Ruth, but it is ridiculous. I tell you what though, if you find him, pass on my address would you? I could do with a new cleaner."

"I don't have your address."

The words are out before I can stop them, coated in a tone that has nothing to do with Mr Walden.

"I knew it."

"What?"

"This is all about you trying to get my attention. You want me to feel sorry for you so I'll spend more time with you, don't you?"

"No."

"At least have the balls to admit it."

"Honestly Paul, I swear. I'm scared."

"You're paranoid, that's what you are. I can't come running every time you forget what colour flowers you buy. I have a job to do. I have a life."

"So do I."

The only convincing thing about those three words is their meekness.

"In that case, go and live it and stop looking for things to be neurotic about. And I would seriously scrap the idea of getting the police involved. You'd be wasting their time."

I consider telling him about Walden's reference to *Jane Eyre*. But I'm sure he would find an alternative explanation. For whatever reason, Paul has decided that I don't feature in the same book that James believes was written for me and me only.

- 26 -

James Hunter had never felt used after sex. But that was before Ruth. After leaving the bed they had shared for such a short time, he walked along the windswept promenade, replaying the events of the evening and yearning to be back by her side.

The intimacy between them up there, high above sea level, had left him puzzled. Surely she had encouraged his advances. She hadn't protested when he ran his fingers over her sad face, nor resisted when he had undressed her. And although she had been a quiet rather than a passionate lover, she had not led him to believe she was unhappy at the way the evening had progressed. His only regret was his performance. He knew he could do better than he had, and put his shortcoming down to the feelings of fascination and intimidation she stirred in him. He had wanted to apologise, but it seemed so adolescent, so he had followed her lead and simply lain in silence.

She had not done as other women do and snuggled her head into his chest, but had moved far enough away from him to let him know she no longer cared to share her bed with him. He knew he had not satisfied her, and her distance had suggested she was not going to offer him a second chance. She had been the first to speak, and had made it clear in stating how late it must be, that it was time for James to leave. His suggestion that they keep in touch by trying together to figure out what the book was all about, which was the best thing he could think of at the time, had been received with flat thanks.

As the night thinned, he had returned to find out all he could about Ruth in his grandly named customer database, which was in fact no more than an old filing cabinet. Her registration form, which dated back to 2003, told him she lived in Essex, worked in London for a company he had never heard of, but concluded from the name had something to do with hair, and was a Ms rather than a Mrs. An evasive title, he thought, but one that allowed him to hope that she was not married.

It also told him she preferred reading fiction to non-fiction, and the list of books he had dispatched to her over the years confirmed this predilection. Once he had found out all he could from the tatty document, he looked up the exact location of her town and allowed his imagination to carry him the hundreds of miles to her front door.

The thought of that front door and the woman who lived behind it had been at the forefront of his mind for the day and a half that had passed since slipping back into his clothes in the en-suite of Room 539. He hoped the memory would find its way into the mental file he called "dalliances', but it was showing no sign of being thus confined. Quite the opposite in fact.

On the few occasions that his phone rang, James would pounce on it. Every time he saw a woman of Ruth's stature, he quickened his pace, and whenever he heard the merest trace of a Scottish accent, he spun around to look for her.

Had she been an ordinary holidaymaker, he might have found it easier to stop thinking about her, but that was not the case. She had come to him for a specific reason and, although she had disappeared back to her own life, her reason for making the journey up north remained with him, He was involved in the Walden plot too. By design, no less, and therefore felt no guilt at having photocopied the whole of *The Ruthlessness of One Man* when she had left it in his office.

James found the book and its floral prose too sickly, but the more he read, the more he felt compelled to plough through it. He wanted to see Davina become something greater than the lonely and manipulative woman she had been drawn as. He wanted to believe she was like the woman he had held in his arms so recently, and not vice versa.

He actively disliked Tod Walden, who turned up uninvited almost everywhere Davina went, determined to share with her the benefit of his apparently endless wisdom on life and the way she ought to lead hers. His biggest objection to the male protagonist, however, was that he felt like romantic competition. That being so, James wanted to find out who had created him, and what part he hoped to play in Ruth's life.

The main hurdle to achieving that goal was that he didn't know Ruth well enough to be able to decide which references were potentially significant. He diligently took notes as he read, compiling a list of mentions he either knew were, or thought might be, of relevance. These included *Jane Eyre*, a scheming mother, a Tupperware lunchbox, a privet hedge, and a married lover called Thor who, by page 60, looked set to bear the brunt of Walden's increasingly menacing wrath.

- 2 7 -

*W*hat Davina ought, after several months of Thursday evening meetings, to have been able to work out for herself, was that Thor was married, and therefore an entirely unsuitable mate. In courting a man already bound by conjugal vows, she was not only compromising her own suitability as a candidate for life-long happiness, but was playing a major role in an unforgivable act of betrayal.

Davina had spent much of her life with her head buried in the white sands of Iona, and saw no immediate need to change her ways. Yet clearly there was a need, and if she was not prepared to satisfy it, then Tod was more than prepared to do it for her. He was happy to be the one to put an end to the weekly agreement which saw Thor knock at her door, neatly hang his Saville Row suit over her bedroom chair, ravage her, and then put it back on before returning to his nuptial bed.

Tod had seen enough of Davina's general state of loneliness to know she would not take well to her lover suddenly disappearing from her life with no prior warning, and therefore decided to inform her of the blindingly obvious, and of its inevitable fallout.

Unbeknownst to Davina, on the final Thursday of her affair, Tod met her from the train and walked behind her as she trod her usual path home. He followed her into the supermarket where she stopped to buy herself a microwave meal in order not to have to have sex on an empty stomach, and a bottle of wine in order to overcome the inhibitions that tried to prevent her having it at all.

It was while she was in the frozen foods aisle that he moved, subtly of course, into her line of vision. He watched the slow dawning of recognition fill her features and waited for her advance towards him.

"Hello Mr Walden. What a lovely surprise!'
"Please call me Tod."
"What are you doing here, Tod?"
"It's a small world, Davina."
"But what brings you to this corner of it?"
"I always shop here."
"Really?"
"Yes."
"I've never seen you here before."
"But I have seen you."
"Have you?"
 She stared at him for a long moment, smiling shyly.
"Yes. I see you here every Thursday night before your visitor comes."
"My visitor?"
"Come, come Davina, we both know who I'm talking about. Do you never spare a thought for Thor's wife?"
"Who's Thor?"
"We both know who Thor is."
"I don't."
"Who is the wine for?"
"Me."
"You alone?"
"No."
"No. The wine is for you and Thor, and Thor is your lover, your lover who comes to visit you every Thursday evening."
"His name is not Thor. It is Paul."
"I would prefer to call him Thor. Are you aware he is standing in the way of your happiness?"
"No."
"Or that he is married?"
"No he isn't."
"Oh, but he is. And are you aware that he has twins?"
"No he doesn't."
"Oh, but he does. And are you aware that he has to go?"
"Go?"
"Yes, go."
"Where to?"
"Leave that to me."

- 2 8 -

Paul's visit ended soon after I told him about the well-made bed to which he previously hinted we should retire for a while. He left me with the knowledge that my paranoia, as he calls it, is too much for him. So here I am, alone again but for echoes of my conversation with Paul and traces of what I saw when I came home from Scarborough.

The more I think about it now, the less able I am to remember about what I really did with the wine glasses. As for the bed, perhaps it didn't look any different to the way it usually does. One thing I'm certain about, however, is that I didn't buy a white flower, and as much as I would like to think it possible, I know that colour doesn't fade from petals overnight.

This house, which has long offered me protection from the outside world, now feels hostile. The familiar sounds it makes in the night are infested with danger.

If I knew where to go to, I would leave. Right now. I would just pack my bags and get away from this place I know has been touched by hands that don't belong here. But the only place I could realistically go is to my mother's house, and that is too far away. In every sense.

I can imagine her response to me telling her about Walden. She'd say she warned me, and that if I have been written into a sinister book it's my own fault for not listening to her warnings about living in a place where the streets are lined with peril. Until now I've seen none of it, but she believes what she wants to believe and will never know the reality, because not once in all the years I've been gone has she so much as suggested coming to visit me. And when I go to see her, she reproaches me for living so far away, for not going home more often, for not telling her more about my life.

Self-pity is beckoning, but I've been seduced by it often enough before to know it can offer no refuge. I know what I have to do.

You see me Walden, I'm getting up. Come and make my bed if you want to. I'm not doing it. I'm running a bath. I'm cleaning myself of you. I'm not going to let you frighten me out of my own life.

*

It's strange going back to work, to walk with, yet without, the same people to the station. Some nod or smile in recognition of our shared path, others don't bother. Any one of them could be Walden. It could be the man in the hat who has just walked past me, or whoever it is that is keeping pace right behind me.

I go into the newsagents just outside the station entrance, pick up a newspaper, and take it to man at the counter, his cream turban moving with him as he nods at me.

"Just the paper, dear?"

"Yes thanks."

"Have you been on holiday…?"

Our conversation doesn't usually venture this far.

"Me?"

"…I haven't seen you for a couple of days. Have you been away?"

"I… I just, well, I just had a couple of days off."

"You have a good time?"

He gives me my change. I find it hard, given the sheer numbers of customers who go into his shop every day, to believe he noticed my absence. But it seems that he did.

"I… Yes, thank you. Not bad."

*

My desk and the objects on it - the computer, the stapler, the post-it notes, and the dusty cactus - are all exactly where I left them. No stalker has been tampering here. Everything looks the same, yet different in the context of the life I've been leading, or perhaps the life that has been leading me, since I last sat here. I don't know if it's because of Walden or James, or neither, or both, but, as I stare at my desk, the ambivalence I've felt about my job since I began it years earlier crystallises into a picture of clear and perfect dislike.

I'm so lost in my thoughts that I don't notice Hazel until she is next to me.

"Ruth… there you are. We were starting to think you'd left us for good."

She smiles at me.

"Glad to have you back."

Whether she means it or not, my need for allies allows me choose to believe she is serious. That same need makes me agree to her suggestion that I join her and my other colleagues for lunch in the local pub.

We get drinks, order food, and push our way through the sea of white-collar workers to a table at the back of the pub. I end up next to a woman from accounting who looks like she wishes I hadn't.

"We were lucky to get a seat." My words thud onto the table in front of us.

"This is nothing," the woman, whose name I know is Sally, assures me. "You're Ruth, aren't you?"

"Yes. That's right."

I'm astonished she knows my name.

"I like your coat."

I look at my coat to assess whether or not she is likely to be joking.

"It's really nice."

"Thanks. It's old."

"Oh."

Sally turns to talk to the woman at her other side, leaving me to fend for myself. I retreat into my thoughts, which whisk me back to the table I sat at in Scarborough, with the man I had planned to call today to ask politely if he could go and retrieve the book from our hotel. I can feel him and see him lying on top of me, holding my face in his hands. The rough edges of the memory are rendered smooth by the awkwardness of the here and now, and James becomes someone trusted and solid. I like what I did with James. And I like him too.

Imagining he is watching me, I lean forward and try to become involved in a conversation between Hazel and our temp, Amanda. They're discussing holiday plans. I nod and make noises to suggest I'm interested. Though I'm unlikely to go to any of the places on their lists.

"Are you going anywhere, Ruth?"

"She never goes anywhere. Do you, Ruth?" Hazel answers for me as though we were best friends.

"I might go home. To Scotland."

"Do your parents still live there?"

"Just my mum."

"Are they divorced?"

"Her father's dead."

Amanda doesn't know whether to look at me or Hazel, the bearer of my sad tidings. In the end, her eyes meet mine.

"I'm sorry." She looks like she means it.

"It was a long time ago."

"Do you have any brothers and sisters?"

"No, it's just me and my mother. She runs a B&B up there. But I might be going to Yorkshire as well." I don't know where the words, or indeed the thought came from.

"Yorkshire and Scotland. Sounds like a blast." Hazel does a poor job of disguising her sarcasm, which Amanda ignores as she presses me for more information.

"Where in Yorkshire?"

"Scarborough."

"I've never been there. Have you got family there too?"

"No. A friend."

I don't need to look at Hazel to know I've hooked her interest.

"A friend, huh? What kind of friend? Is it a man?"

"Hazel, you're so blunt…"

"Ruth doesn't mind. Do you?"

I say nothing, because I'm not sure what to say. My silence floats across the table to where Hazel pounces upon it, remoulding it to suit her.

"You've got a boyfriend up there, haven't you? In Scarrrrrborough?"

However little I protest, I know it will be too much, so I just shake my head.

"Don't be shy. What's his name?"

It seems as if everyone around the table has stopped talking and is now looking at me.

"We're all dying to know," Hazel insists.

I doubt that.

"We thought you might be a lesbian, see…"

The blood rushes to my face.

"So come on then, what's his name?"

Hazel has me cornered. If I tell her I don't have a boyfriend in Scarborough I'll fuel their belief that I prefer women. But if I do tell her, I'll have to make up a relationship that doesn't exist. Or tell her about the book. She's staring at me, waiting for an answer, when Amanda points at my bag.

"Is that you, Ruth?"

It is. My phone that seldom rings is ringing now. The display says "Paul". Hazel is sitting close enough and is indiscreet enough to see it too.

"Ooo, I think his name is Paul," she announces to one and all.

I shake my head and stand up. I don't want to talk to him with everyone staring at me, so I start through the crowds towards the door before I pick up.

"Hello Paul, what a lovely surprise."

"You've got to be kidding me."

I'm almost at the door where a group of women are screeching with laughter.

"Sorry? I can't hear you that well. Just a moment."

"Where the hell are you?"

"Out having lunch."

"You're unbelievable."

The fury in his voice cuts through the noise of the pub. I hurry past the women onto the street.

"Sorry about that. I'm outside now. It's nice to hear from you."

"Don't even think about playing dumb with me."

"What?"

"You heard me. I might have known you'd pull a stunt like that. Selfish fucking bitch."

"Paul! What are you talking about?"

"I'm talking about you being home-wrecking little slut."

My instincts are screaming at me to put the phone down, but I can't.

"What?"

"I'm talking about you being a two-faced slag."

Big tears are welling.

"I… I don't understand what you –"

"Don't come all little Miss Naïve with me. You know exactly what I'm talking about."

A woman smoking a cigarette smiles at me. I keep my eyes on her for balance.

"I'll tell you this though. You don't win, Ruth. You lose. Worse than that, we all fucking lose."

His voice sounds as wobbly as my legs feel. Whatever is going on, we're in it together.

"Paul, please tell me what's happened. Perhaps I can help."

He laughs. A bitter laugh.

"You've ruined my marriage. That's what's happened."

"Your what?"

"You heard me, my marriage!'

"But I… but you… I didn't know…'

"Don't bullshit me Ruth."

The woman with the cigarette has stubbed it. I'm staring at her, but she has forgotten I exist. She goes back into the pub, leaving me alone with Paul.

"Don't tell me you didn't know I was married, because I know you did. All that crap the other night about that stupid book, it was just you trying to get me to admit I have a wife."

"No. You have to believe me. I had no idea."

"I should have known you'd go snooping. I should have guessed that someone as self-obsessed as you would want to know everything about me."

"Paul! Stop it!" Whatever has been holding my tears back now gives way to their mounting pressure. They clog my throat and my nose in their hurry to see the light of day.

"What the fuck have you got to cry about? You haven't lost anything. You don't have anything to lose. You're just a sad, lonely little girl who goes around ruining innocent, decent lives. I have kids you know. Kids. Of course you know. You know everything."

"No! I didn't… I don't… children?"

I catch my reflection in the pub window. It's a blurred mess. Beyond it, I can make out Hazel walking towards me. I hurry around the corner. She can't be allowed to see me like this.

"Of course I have children. You think a man like me has nothing more in his life than a weekly shag on the side? Because that is all you were for me, and you weren't even a very good one."

"What… what are you… how can you say that?"

"Because it's true. You are a crap fuck. And you're outrageous, sending your messenger round to my house to tell my wife I've been screwing you. It's not only outrageous, it's pathetic, it's…"

He's shouting now. I am leaning into the wall. I can't take the weight of this by myself. "…fucking mental. My kids were there. How do you think they felt when some old man walks up to their front door and tears their lives apart?"

"What are you talking about? What old man?"

"The old man you sent round to my house to shatter my family."

"But I didn't. I wouldn't. Please Paul, you've got it all wrong. I don't know what you're talking about. You have to believe me."

I can hear Hazel shouting my name somewhere in the background, but I don't care. I slide down the wall and crouch on the ground among the peed out Friday night cocktails and old cigarette butts.

"I don't believe a word you say."

I'm trying to order my thoughts, but they're piling up on top of each other.

"I don't know any old men. I don't even know where you live. None of this makes sense."

He falls quiet.

"I mean it Paul. Whoever came to your house had nothing to do with me."

"Oh Jesus, you really are a fuck-up. How can you deny it? I'm telling you, my wife spoke to him. He told her you sent him because you wanted her to know we were having an affair."

Now it is me who is quiet.

"Which means she knows. She knows something that wasn't fucking worth knowing, and definitely wasn't worth doing. I could tell you were weird, but I didn't think you'd go that far. You listen to me, Ruth: you stay away from me and my family, and tell your old man to do the same. I mean it. If you so much as try to phone me, I'll make sure you regret it."

He hangs up.

"Ruth?"

I look up to see Hazel standing a foot or so from where I'm crouched. Her expression suggests she's been there a while. I wipe my face with my sleeve and try to get up. She puts out her hand.

"Boyfriend troubles?"

- 29 -

He is in particularly high spirits this morning, and congratulates himself on a job well done. He considers his actions to be long overdue, and of benefit to all those who stand to be affected by them. He is a great believer in the truth, and is certain it would have surfaced sooner or later, with or without his help.

He has just sat down in his usual place and is in the process of removing the cravat he saves for special occasions, and wore today because he considered it one, when he notices a man turn down her path. He is glad to see it is not Thor, who he sincerely hopes will not be making any more Thursday night visits, but is vexed to note it is the same man from whom he recently saw her hide.

He is not in the mood for a new opponent, *No pen pot! One to contest perhaps? (8)*, but will challenge any new enemy, *Antagonist got me mixed up in Japanese currency deal (5)* he has to.

He takes an instinctive dislike to the visitor, who has the appearance of one who is not to be trusted, and feels himself gearing up for a conflict, *Prisoner and French cop tango – but don't see eye to eye (8)* or *Fight in Sussex? (6)*. All out warfare, *Active conflict brings air force back in Hertfordshire town (7)*, if needs be.

He hastily reties his cravat, smooths his hair and the anger lines around his eyes, walks out of his house, crosses the road, and follows in the footsteps of the stranger to her front door.

He adopts a friendly neighbourhood tone with which to ask the unwanted guest if he requires any help, but is told that he does not. When he pushes the stranger for information on the nature of his call, he learns that Miss Morton has been selected to take part in a census review, and is therefore required to answer questions about various aspects of her life.

He tells the stranger, whose story he is whole-heartedly disinclined to believe, that Miss Morton is out at work, but that she and he are intimately acquainted, so intimately in fact, that he can easily answer any questions on her behalf. He notes the stranger's reluctance to accept the offer of information from anything less than the horse's mouth, but has no intention of letting that stop him from getting what he wants.

In a bid to prove his legitimacy as the aforementioned intimate acquaintance, he opens her front door and invites the stranger inside. He shows him into the kitchen, where he puts on the kettle and leaves it to boil while on the pretence of going to the lavatory. He slips upstairs, opens her wardrobe and fills his lungs with air that smells of the clothes she wears.

- 3 0 -

The further James Hunter read through his pile of photocopied papers, the more concerned he became. Walden's
portrayal of himself hinted at a writer of such irrational
mind that he came close to phoning Ruth to check on her
wellbeing. But each time his fingers twitched with the desire to reach her, he reminded himself he'd have to confess
to having made a copy of her book, a liberty he feared
might not recommend him to her. And if there was one
thing he wanted, it was to remain recommendable.

There was another issue too. If Ruth was right and
Walden genuinely was incorporating aspects of her real life
into his depiction of Davina, then she might, regardless of
their night together, already be romantically involved. Al-
beit with a married man.

He was well aware of the absurdity of being jealous of
her alter ego's illusory lover, but somehow he couldn't help
it. And as hard as he tried, he could not get her or her en-
tourage of characters out of his mind. He tried to talk them,
drink them and walk them away, but they did not want to
go. And so, on the third night after his one with Ruth, he
turned to another woman to help him back into the here and
now.

The woman in question was a holidaymaker from Liverpool who'd taken a shine to him the moment he walked
through the door of his local, and who shared his desire to
spend a few hours away from reality. For the most part they
succeeded, although had she known him just a little better,
she would have noticed the wistful look that crossed his

face when, every now and then, he glanced at a table towards the back of the pub.

Just before midnight, with his skin uncomfortably full of liquor and the Liverpudlian on his arm, he walked out onto the prom. Stumbling along it together, he felt pitifully lonely, so when she invited him back to her boarding house for a nightcap, he was happy to accept. More, however, out of a desire to put Ruth to bed than to take her replacement to it.

When he woke in the early morning, it took James a few moments to recognise his surroundings. The paper peeling in the corners where the walls met the ceiling was as unfamiliar to him as the smell of the sheets on the bed in which he instinctively remembered he was not alone.

He turned his head to see the woman asleep at his side, and knew in an instant that rather than helping him move beyond Ruth, she had pushed him closer towards her. And from there, he knew he had to forget his sense of male pride, and come clean about his feelings. Which in turn would mean finally giving her a call.

- 3 1 -

I didn't go back into the pub after my call with Paul, but to the office where everyone but Hazel has been giving me a wide berth all afternoon. I don't know what she told them; possibly that I'm the psycho Paul says I am, the lesbian they thought I was, or that I'm just plain strange, but my being here among them feels as awkward to them as it does me. Hazel has offered to be my listening ear but even if I wanted to tell her what happened I couldn't because I don't understand it.

Paul is married.

His marriage is over because he had an affair with me.

I allegedly sent an old man to tell his wife.

Or so his wife told him.

Which is what he told me.

And none of it makes sense.

I've been over it again and again, looking for a possible explanation, but the only half-way plausible one I can come up with is that a friend of his wife's found out about us and told her. I know it's not the most logical solution, because the friend would need a reason beyond my powers of explanation to send someone else to do the telling rather than doing it herself.

The other interpretation clawing at my brain involves an even more audacious Walden, who not only makes my bed for me, but sees fit to meddle in my private affairs.

"Biscuit Ruth?"

It must be three o'clock. My stomach is too tight for food, but I take one because I need to taste normality.

"Thank you."

"You feeling a bit better now? Men don't know their arses from their elbows. They aren't worth crying about, that's for sure."

There's an easy gaiety to her voice that suddenly makes me want to be somewhere safe.

"I mean it. I mean, I know we've all done it, but they don't deserve it. Go on, have another biscuit, and if there's anything I can do, just shout."

"Okay. There is, actually."

"Yeah?"

"I was wondering if I could take a couple of days off?"

She puts another biscuit in her mouth and pulls a pained face.

"I don't know, Ruth. We've got a lot coming up in the next week or so."

"It wouldn't be for long. I just feel like it would do me good to have a break."

She chokes on her chocolate wafer.

"It would do us all good to have a break. But we can't just go running off when a man behaves like a dick. We'd never get anything done, would we? And let's not forget you just had time off for sickness."

I let her talk about the importance of taking my job seriously and fight versus flight, thinking as she speaks that the latter is the only thing that makes sense.

"I'm a very good listener, Ruth. I could have been a counsellor."

Not mine. As she speaks, I envisage myself getting up and walking out, climbing on the bus, then the train. Not my usual train though, a west coast line that would carry me the length of the country and over the border, to where I would get on another train, and then a ferry, followed by another bus, and a second ferry from which I would see a tiny island in the middle of the wild ocean.

"So if I were you, I'd phone him back and give him a piece of my mind."

"Maybe later," I say knowing I'll never speak to Paul again.

Satisfied, she goes back to her desk, and I to my island. I'm standing on its highest point, taking a deep breath of clean air, staring out to the sea all around when the ring of my phone brings me back to the limits of my office surroundings. Hazel instantly turns around to look at me, her face burning with hopeful curiosity.

"Looks like he beat you to it."

The phone on my desk is ringing, and I can see from the display that it's not Paul.

"Aren't you going to answer? It might be him calling to apologise."

I don't want to answer. I'm afraid to. Because what if it is Walden? What if he really was the one who told Paul's wife about us? If he could do that, I'm sure he could get hold of my telephone number.

"Go on Ruth, pick it up."

I can't. If it is him, the thin layer of glue holding me together will dissolve and everyone in this office, not just Hazel, will be forced to bear witness to more of the real me than they could cope with. I pick up the phone and press the reject button.

"Too late."

Hazel's back is half-turned towards me when the ringing starts up again.

"Blimey, I'll say this for him, he's persistent."

This time I don't even pretend, I simply turn the phone off.

- 3 2 -

He is having a good day. He has something he didn't have before he met the stranger on her path and is pleased with himself for his methods of extraction. He saw her mobile telephone number on the man's notepad, and memorised it before telling the stranger it was incorrect, and subsequently giving him an all new, but correctly incorrect contact for her. He does not expect the stranger to make a repeat visit.

He has also dealt with Thor. Thor, he is sure, will not be coming back, and this is a great success, *Search after trick to vanquish the foe (8)*. He is extremely happy about all these things. Thor, because Thor deserves to be dead. The stranger, because he too has no business being with or anywhere near her. And the phone number because is it one thing that has eluded him since the very first time he broke into her house to borrow the spare key from which to cut the one he has been using ever since.

His various searches through her home easily led him to conclude her love of a Brontë classic, her enjoyment of books in general, and her membership of the Bicycle Book Club, but had always failed to yield the eleven digits he has now committed to a warm place in his memory. A triumph, *Mechanical herald in great victory (7)*, that will assure him even greater access to her, which, as she will soon understand, is all either of them really need.

He phones her.

He is not planning to reveal his identity - that is something she must work out for herself - but to hide his number behind technology and his voice behind that of a market researcher telephoning to question her about the books she has read lately.

He is irritated that she doesn't answer and even more so that she does not offer her callers a recorded message. In that respect, her home phone is a superior experience.

He sits at his desk, the photographs of her smiling up at him submissively, and he works. He can still feel the positive effects of his day's conquest, *Such endless organized religion meets Gestapo to fulfil objective (7)*, but he can feel something else, too. Doubt has come to rest on his shoulder, and is whispering to him that he should have found out the real identity of the tall stranger without whom there would have been no achievement, *A Companion of Honour that is, without His Excellency, vehement in claiming result (11)*.

- 3 3 -

When Morna Morton was told that Ruth was "involved with a substantially older man" she felt a mixture of jealousy that her daughter had failed to tell her, fear that the omission could equate to there being something to hide, and distaste at the idea of any significant age difference.

The investigator had not been able to give the man's exact age, but had said he'd happily "put him in his early sixties." Unable to envisage her daughter on the arm of a man three decades her senior, she had queried the estimate. But her source had insisted it was true, and that he had not only seen the man in question with his own eyes, but had even had coffee and a long talk with him. A talk which had led him, and in turn Morna, to learn that Ruth was seeing a writer of both fiction and non-fiction. As someone who had once thought she might write a book, but had never quite found the confidence to rise to the challenge, Morna felt the profession went some way to compensating for his seniority.

Yet now she was in possession of information for which she was certain she would soon receive a bill, Morna didn't know what to do with it. She only knew what she couldn't do, and that was to confront Ruth with these revelations. Not outright, at least, although there was nothing stopping her from trying to steer their next conversation towards the topic of older men and boyfriends. She only hoped that this Tod Walden, whoever he was, was treating Ruth with the kind of care she would have liked to be treated herself

Thoughts of men, both old and young, kept Morna from her normal chores and at the kitchen table for much of the afternoon, where optimism and pessimism were her revolving guests. As her day turned to night and dreams overtook thought, she found herself playing a delighted grandmother to a little girl who bore a striking resemblance to the one she had tried her best by.

By the time morning rolled around again, the dream child had touched her heart softly enough to fill it with a fear of being denied access to the next generation of her family. Morna didn't know how exactly to prevent that from happening, but she did know she couldn't sit about waiting for Ruth to decide the time had come to mend fences. She was going to have to take decisive action and show her daughter that she was still a part of her life, whether she liked it or not.

She considered inviting Ruth and her partner to come and stay with her, but dismissed the thought on the grounds that it would force her to come clean. The other option was going to visit them.

It would be a surprise. She would just turn up at her daughter's home which, by the sounds of things, she shared with her partner. She couldn't wait to see the look on Ruth's face when she realised she would now have to introduce her to Mr Tod Walden. She'd be embarrassed at having been so secretive but Morna would make no mention of it, thereby silently extending an olive branch that would secure her a part in her daughter's, and perhaps one day a grand-daughter's, future.

Her biggest worry, besides returning to the one place on earth she had vowed to stay away from for evermore, was being sure that Ruth would be home and not away somewhere on the day of her arrival. In order to give herself some peace on that front, she settled on a date and, breaking her rule only to make calls to mobile telephones in an emergency, she phoned Ruth's with a flimsy excuse in place.

Her first call went unanswered but, since it was mid-afternoon, she assumed Ruth would be working and thought little of it. She hung up without leaving a message, and tried again an hour or so later, but again it just rung out. By the third attempt, she felt worry taking hold. Ruth could be ignoring her on purpose or, worse still, she might have decided to cut all ties.

When she retired again that night, Moran fell on her knees, pledging to do whatever it would take to become and stay a real part of her daughter's life again. For a second chance, she would, she promised, be a shining example of everything a mother could be.

It was late when her eyes finally closed over her worry, and this time her dreams did not serve up visions of her future grandchild, but of her dead father. When she heard a banging outside, she sleepily handed him a hammer with which to mend the kitchen shelves she had been meaning to tackle herself. As the deceased worked, the banging grew louder and more persistent and was accompanied by shouts of "Mum, wake up, open the door."

- 34 -

The air is so clear and fresh that merely inhaling it is not enough. I want to be it. One of the fishermen hands me a mug of warm tea. I try to thank him but gratitude and relief have rolled a lump into my throat, and all I can get out is a croak. His attention is too tangled in the string of nets for him to notice, and I suddenly envy him his life. A life I know nothing about besides what I see right here, right now. Perhaps I should fish. I would love to spend my days on these mystical waters, far away from Paul and Walden and the phone call I never made to James. Far away from London, from my unhomely home, from thought itself. I would float happily upon the charmed expanse which stretches before me, my very essence buoyed up by the experience.

I sip my tea as the islands through which the boat is tugging forth rise up around me, their beauty as intact as ever. I think ahead to my island, to its worn track that will lead me to where I'm going, to the faded red front door I've pushed open so many times.

I can't believe I'm now so close, can't believe my own spontaneity, my asking the fishermen to take me across the water. Yet I can't imagine anything else. The office I left at the normal time last night is now so distant. It won't miss me any more than I'll miss it.

"You're lucky we could take you all the way across, you'd have had a heck of a wait for the bus over Mull..."

The fisherman is behind me.

"I know. Thank you."

"Eh, no bother to us, we're coming out here anyway." The fisherman smiles at me. I smile back, enjoying the sound of his voice and the honest wear and tear of his face.

"But it's awful unusual for a girl like you to be wanting to get to Iona at the crack of dawn. You must be in a hurry to say your prayers."

He disguises his curiosity with a laugh, and I'm tempted to tell him the whole story. But I can see Iona and its abbey approaching in the distance, so make a note of his comment and a pact with myself to do as he inadvertently suggested.

I climb out of the boat, sketching prayers in my head as I start to walk along the track that always seems lined with them. It's still early and there's not much sign of life, but mine is returning to me, as if my organs and senses have been asleep and suddenly woken filled with renewed vigour. They are in tune with every blade of grass, every daisy and every stone, which together seem to be welcoming me home, assuring me the protection I've travelled all night to find.

I hope my mother will offer me the same.

By the time I reach the door, which is no longer red but green, misgivings are beginning to surface. My mother and I don't have the easiest of relationships. She never misses an opportunity to tell me I should leave London and move closer to home. I sometimes think that's the only reason I've stayed there so long. To make us both unhappy. But I'm here now. I'll tell her she's right and I was wrong. I'll tell her I've come in search of a safe haven. I try the front door, which she generally leaves open, and am surprised to find it locked. I knock but she doesn't answer. Again, a little louder. She must be there, she never goes away. Still no answer. An image of her injured or dead comes to me, but I push it away because surely someone would have informed me. I bang at the door, but still she doesn't come. Maybe she has gone away. Then what will I do? I'm hammering on it now, fear rising high inside me.

"Mum, wake up, open the door!"

*

I'm in. We're together at the kitchen table, drinking tea. She's wearing a flannel nightdress that ages her beyond her years. Her hair, which is now as much grey as red, has grown longer and thinner and is sticking out in all directions, showing me more of her scalp than I want to see. The wrinkles around her mouth have deepened and she looks smaller, thinner. It's only been a year, or perhaps a little more, since I was last here, but she looks different.

She's stunned to see me – stunned and happy. Ecstatic almost and despite my resolve not to let our old patterns of behaviour characterise this visit, I'm wary of that ecstasy.

I sit across from her and lean back into the old wooden armchair. It creaks grudgingly. My mother smiles at me with a softness I don't recognize in her and I wonder if it's a sign that her mind is going the same way. I wrap myself in a blanket, aware that she's staring. To avoid having to meet her eye, green like mine, I pick up the newspaper which is just within arm's reach. It's open at the crossword page, which is a relief. I need to see that some things haven't changed. The first clue listed is *condition to add monster home to future first person*, which I can see at a glance she has answered as *Illness*.

"I still can't believe you're here."

"Well, I am."

"And you really got a taxi all the way from Glasgow to Oban?"

"There were no trains until morning. I'd have had to wait in the station all night."

"Surely you could have found a place to stay? Not that I'm not glad you're here, because I am glad. Ever so glad…"

She leans in towards me. Her proximity makes me nervous, so I keep my eyes on the newspaper. *Eternity in a cod for example – that's a few degrees over (8)*.

"…but you must have more money than sense."

That's more like the mother I know. We're on safe ground now.

"I'd have had to pay for a room if I'd stayed over."

"Aye, but not so much, surely. Anyway, all that matters is that you're here. And you must be exhausted, you poor thing."

Poor thing? Those two words take me back into the un-known, to her growing older, morphing into something I don't recognise, into a grandchildless grandmother, who, my instincts tell me, I have to protect. It's perhaps the first time ever that we've both needed the same thing.

"Why don't you go on upstairs and have a wee sleep?"

Although I should be tired, I'm not.

She gets up and comes over to me.

"I'm sure it'd do you good."

She strokes my shoulder. Lightly. Almost as if she's not touching it at all.

"The bed's all made up."

I get up to go. Because there's something painful about being back in this old kitchen with the vulnerability of my mother in her old person's nightwear.

- 3 5 -

He is not amused. He has phoned her countless times and spent the entire night waiting for her to appear. To no avail. He has just returned from her house where he looked for some indication as to why she should suddenly disappear, *New pears paid for but no longer visible (9)*. Again, to no avail. All he knows is that she has gone, *Departed for Geordieland after his turn (4)*.

He is pacing his front room. With each step he takes, he grows hotter under the collar. His irritation is a result of her sudden erraticism, but is aggravated by his failure to have taken care of the fraudulent census office worker while the chance had been his for the taking.

He picks up the cravat, which he discarded on the floor hours ago, and snaps it tight between his hands. He does not like to be kept waiting. He has waited long enough. From the first moment he saw her, and much longer still.

He does not understand why she has not yet come to knock on his door. He knows she reads books at a steady pace. He has seen the rate at which they are placed upon and then removed from her bedside table, and would expect her to have finished his slim volume by now, and to have understood what it is telling her. He would not have expected her to simply vanish, *Can't be seen in caravan I share (6)*.

He looks out of his window to her empty living room and demands of the air in his own to bring her back from wherever she is. He tells it, and an imaginary her, that he will not tolerate such spontaneous behaviour. He wants to know where she it at all times. That is his right. He does not think she is with Thor, but does have his doubts about the other man - the census impostor - who he believes entirely capable of having kidnapped her, *Youngster slept while taken (9)*. The irony is not lost on him.

Continuing his monologue and snapping his cravat with fury, he tells the absent stranger that he does not know what he's getting into and that, if he values his life in the slightest, he will keep his hands well away from Davina Law.

- 36 -

It's late afternoon by the time I wake up and remember where I am. My room hasn't changed a bit since my last visit. The same white walls bear the same cheesy prints I put up when I was a teenager, and my old pine wardrobe stands guard over the twin beds mum put in when she started her B&B. I sometimes fantasized about bringing Paul here to see my home, about us moving the beds together so we could snuggle up and listen to the wind and the rain that would almost certainly come to welcome us.

Even as I'm walking down the narrow stairs, I'm aware of my reluctance to keep going. I know the feeling well, but this time it's not a fear of the unspoken tension that has lived between us since I can remember that slows me down, but of its no longer being there. Of her age having dissolved it. I tread carefully so as to keep my descent from her for as long as possible, and then hover at the kitchen door, willing her not to be wearing day clothes cut for ancient ladies, or to be shuffling about in saggy tartan slippers.

"Ru-uth?"

I retreat two steps up the wooden staircase.

"Yes?"

She's opened the kitchen door.

"I thought I heard you. Come and sit yourself down."

I'm relieved to see her dressed in a perfectly normal pair of jeans and her hair tied back. But her shirt has a kind of housecoat quality, which fuels my concern about the gallop of her advancing years.

"Thanks."

"You had a good sleep! You've been up there for hours. I thought about coming in and waking you, because you don't want to sleep so much that you'll have to spend all night tonight tossing and turning. But then I decided to leave you to it. You must need it."

"I was pretty tired."

"I'm not surprised, travelling all night like that. You were up there for hours, you know."

She just said that.

"I know."

"Sit yourself down. I'm making a shepherd's pie for dinner. Is that all right for you?"

"That's fine. I'm starving."

"How about some tea and a piece of shortbread to keep you going?"

"Thanks."

I sit, my head still full of sleep, and watch her as she pours me a cup of tea. I'm sure her hand is shaking. She takes the chair next to mine and strokes my hair as if I were a small child and she were someone other than herself. I don't mean to, but I shrink back.

"So are you going to tell me what made you come up here? I mean it's a lovely surprise, and you're very welcome, but for the life of me, I can't work out what I did to deserve the honour."

There she is, my real mother fighting to get to the surface.

"What's so funny?"

"Nothing."

"Doesn't look like nothing."

There she is again.

"I just thought it was about time I came to see you."

"I see. No special reason then?"

"I just needed to get away."

"Needed?"

She's giving me an opening, but now I'm here in this kitchen on this island, the last thing I want to talk about is Walden. I could stay here. Not in her house, but here, on Iona. I could just move my life back here, never even go and collect my things.

"Yeah."

"Have you been working too hard?"

"Maybe."

"I'm surprised you didn't call first though."

"It was all a bit spur of the moment."

"You're lucky I don't have any guests at the moment. You'd have had to sleep on the sofa or get in with me."

"That was lucky."

Very lucky.

She's hovering about in the background now, clattering pans and crockery as she speaks.

"Come on then, tell me how you are and what you've been up to. I want to hear it all."

"I haven't been up to anything much really. Just work."

"Have you been working too hard?"

Didn't she just ask me that?

"I don't know."

"Well you shouldn't work too hard, it's not good for you. You need to make sure you get some pleasure out of life, have some fun. I expect you go out a lot too, don't you?"

"I… errm…"

"No need to look at me like that, Ruth Morton. You're not a child anymore, you don't need my permission to go out."

"I know… It's just…'

"I expect you're always out on dates, or whatever they call them these days."

"On dates?"

"Isn't that what you say?"

"I suppose so."

"I thought so. See, I'm still with it… So do you? Bet you're fighting men off with a stick."

This is moving from the unusual to the uncomfortable.

"I'm not fighting anyone off."

"Och well, never mind. You only need one anyway."

"Shall I set the table, mum?"

"No need yet, dear. It'll be another hour or so before we're that far on. You just stay where you are and keep talking to me. It's not often I get to make a fuss of you… So is there one?"

"One what?"

"One man?"

"Mu-um."

"I'm only asking. You're getting to the age now where… well, you know, where all the good ones are married?"

And the bad ones.

"Do we have to talk about this?"

"Not if you don't want to."

"Good. So how have you been?"

She looks up from setting the table, and takes hold of one of my hands.

"Me? Oh fine. It's you I'm worried about."

"Me? Why?"

"It's just that… I'd hate to think you were staying single because that's what you learned from me."

"I'm not."

"No?"

"No."

"You're not single or you're not following my single example?"

"I'm fine, okay? I don't really want to talk about this."

"Suit yourself. But if you're just going to sit there in silence, it wouldn't hurt you to get up and lend me a hand."

Morna Morton had never had her prayers answered so quickly before. When she'd finally recognised that the banging in her dream was happening in reality, and had opened the door, her first reaction was to look into the half-light of the sky in disbelief. Her second was to silently reiterate her pledge to outdo her previous parenting with a brand sweet enough to make her daughter really want a mother in her life.

She didn't know how He had completed his work so fast, but was glad He had chosen to do so on a night she was wearing her new nightdress. She had felt presentable. Which was more, she acknowledged, than could be said of her daughter. Granted, Ruth had had a long night and had arrived tired to the bone, but nonetheless Morna had found her looking drawn and pale, and had instantly doubted whether a relationship with a man almost twice her age agreed with her.

But that was evidently not something Ruth was willing to talk about. Likewise her reason for having turned up in the wee small hours. In fact she seemed unwilling to talk about anything much besides the details of her trip.

Ruth's huggermuggery made it difficult for Morna to be the mother the heavens, having delivered her daughter home safely, now expected her to be. She would have liked to insist that Ruth tell her what she in fact already knew, or at the very least to steer the conversation towards the subject of age gaps in relationships. But in the spirit of kindliness, she refrained, and instead concentrated her energies on creating an atmosphere of warmth and loving,

even going so far as to stroke her daughter's hair in a gesture she was sure felt as unnatural to Ruth as it did to her.
But a promise was a promise. And a promise to God was
more.

- 38 -

I'm watching my mother mash the potatoes, standing close by, but not too close, wondering what I should offer to do next. She moves about the kitchen in a way that doesn't invite help. She's annoyed with me for not telling her what she wants to know, but what can I say? No, mother, I'm not in a relationship. I thought I was, but it turned out he was married. Only he didn't tell me about it until my stalker - yes you heard me right, my stalker - who, incidentally, wrote a book about me, for me, and about me, chased him out of town.

"Are you just going to stand there in silence?"

"No. What can I do to help?"

"You can peel some apples for a crumble."

I'm glad of something to do.

"So how have things been on the island? Any interesting news from anyone?"

"No, not really. The most interesting thing that'll have happened in a while will be your surprise return. Nobody will know what to make of that."

"I don't suppose anyone will be that interested."

"Of course they will. But I don't know what to tell them when they ask why you are here."

"Don't tell them anything. I just wanted to come home for a while."

"For a while? How long is a while?"

"I don't know. A week, maybe two. If that's all right with you."

"Of course it is."

Her face has lit up and a surge of warmth passes between us.

"I've got a booking next week though, so we'll need to see where you sleep then."

"Okay."

We work side-by-side in contented silence; me with the apples, her with the potatoes. Just like any other mother and daughter. Now feels like the kind of moment such other daughters might choose to confide in their other mothers. But I'm not sure enough of us yet to try.

"What do you like to do in your spare time? Do you go to the cinema, or the theatre?"

"Sometimes."

"And do you still read? You always loved books so much."

"Yes, I still read a lot."

"What are you reading at the moment?"

"Actually I'm not reading anything just now. I'm taking a break."

"Another break?"

"What do you mean?"

"A break from work, a break from books…"

"I started a book but didn't like it and I haven't begun a new one yet. That's all."

"I see. Well, I read a review of a book the other day. I don't remember the title, but it sounded very good. It was by someone called Tod something or other. Tod Woden… or Walden. At least I think it was."

I look over at her. Her head is down, her eyes on her potatoes.

"What did you just say? Tod Walden?"

"Yes, it was Walden. I'm pretty sure. Do you know his books?"

"What did you read about him?"

"A review. But don't ask me the name of the book because I can't remember."

"Where did you read it?"

"Och, I don't recall that."

"Was it in a newspaper?"

"I don't think so."

"Well where then?"

"Don't ask me. My memory's not what it used to be."

"Don't you have any idea?"

"I suppose it must have been in a paper... although maybe it was in a magazine at the dentist. I was over there a couple of weeks ago."

"Which magazine?"

"I don't know which ones they have, I just flick through them. I never look at the titles. You seem awful interested. Are you particularly fond of this Walden man's books then?"

My mind is racing. If there is a review about him then he must exist as a writer, which mean other people know about him, which means... I don't know what it means, but it must mean something.

"No."

She casts me a look of suspicion.

"You could have fooled me. You're more excited now than I've seen you for a long time."

It's another opening. I could tell her everything, and part of me wants to. But if she has read about him in a magazine at a dentist on the island of Mull, that could render everything I could say utterly obsolete, and I don't want to confuse her.

"The article made him sound very intelligent."

"It was an article?"

"I already told you that."

"You said it was a review."

"Same difference."

"No it's not. Was it about him or about his book?"

"Both."

I can't believe I've come all this way to get away from Walden and here I am in my mother's tiny island kitchen listening to her tell me what an intelligent man he is.

"What did it say? Which book did it refer to?"

"I told you, I don't remember the name."

"Was it *The Ruthlessness of One Man*...?"

"It might have been. That does ring a faint bell."

"What else did it say?"

"That he was a writer, an older gentleman and that he is in a relationship with a much younger woman. From Scotland, I think it said."

Each of her words is ripe with implication that is too complex for me to fathom.

"Ruth, are you okay? You look a little pale."

"I'm fine."

"Are you sure?"

I nod.

"Well if you're not, or if you need to talk about anything, I'm here for you."

The only thing I want to talk about right now is where she read all this.

- 3 9 -

James Hunter was growing increasingly restless. A full 24 hours had passed since he had stopped trying Ruth's number and instead done the logical thing and left her a message. It was a message he now regretted because, as is the way of such things, it rendered him powerless to get in touch again without seeming desperate. And although he feared that was precisely what he was becoming, he didn't want her to know it.

Every time his phone rang he pounced on it, hoping it would put him out of his growing misery. But so far the only calls to come in were related to the business of selling books, something for which he could currently muster no interest whatsoever. He was behind on processing orders, behind on dispatching those he had processed. And all, ironically enough, because of a book that could not be found on his list.

He had discovered upon continuing his journey through *The Ruthlessness of One Man*, that Tod Walden had not violently done away with Thor, but had slyly removed him from the picture by telling the wife about her husband's philandering ways. Admittedly, he was glad to see the back of the arrogant adulterer, but was again disturbed by the possibility that Davina's story might reflect the truth, because that would make Ruth's stalker very persistent indeed.

It would also imply there was trouble ahead for whoever inspired Walden's character called Shelagh. So much so that he felt a pressing need to find out whether Ruth knew anyone on a remote Scottish island.

- 40 -

When she finally gave in to her urge to casually drop Mr Walden's name into the otherwise stilted conversation with her daughter, Morna was quite unprepared for the response it triggered, and had to think on her toes in order not to be caught out by her own curiosity. She silently praised and envied this Tod Walden for managing, even in his absence, to spark in her daughter a fire of interest, the likes of which she had not witnessed since the days they spent scouring rock pools for signs of sea life.

Fast-tracking through the intervening years of their thinning relationship, she wondered – not for the first time - how things would have evolved if she'd been a less anxious mother.

As she looked at Ruth, who was standing opposite her almost begging for information she couldn't provide, Morna felt a twinge of guilt at having used such devious means to drill into her private sphere. But it was done now. There was no going back and confession was out of the question.

She would ask the heavens for forgiveness, and was sure they would grant it, because they understood that she would never have needed to tell such a fib in the first place if Ruth had not insisted on being so secretive. A habit she perpetuated when not five minutes later she began to make a hoo-ha about needing to find an internet connection.

- 41 -

"I have one in the front room."

"What?"

"An internet."

"What do you mean, 'an internet?'"

"I have a computer."

"Really?"

"Really."

"I didn't know you had one."

"How else d'you think I deal with my B&B bookings?"

"You didn't mention it."

"Didn't I? We don't spend a lot of time talking to one another, so when I do get to speak to you, I'm more interested in knowing about you than yapping about my computer."

"Do you mind if I use it?"

"Go ahead. I'll be through it the kitchen. But mind you don't break it."

"I won't."

As soon as she has left the room, I run a search on 'Tod Walden review', and come up with a number of sites in German. I try 'Walden article', and get a politician, a musician, a criminal, and Henry Thoreau. 'Walden review article magazine' and 'The Ruthlessness of One Man review' are of equally little help. I need my mother to remember where she read what about Walden. I can hear her singing a hymn to herself in the kitchen, and have the distinct feeling that I'm going to get nothing more from her than I already have.

Being careful not to break her computer, I look at my email to see if there's anything from Hazel justifiably berating me for neither turning up today, nor offering a reason for my absence. She has outdone my expectations and sent three mails, the first at 9.40, at which point I was officially only ten minutes late. The second arrived around eleven, and seethes at me from the screen, while the last one, sent just an hour ago, is a little less ferocious.

To: RMorton@BaldNoMore.co.uk
From: HStack@BaldNoMorec.co.uk
Subject: Where ARE you??

Ruth

It is now almost five o'clock, and you are still not here. I've tried calling you dozens of times, both at home and on your mobile and this is my third email today. Where the hell are you? I can't decide if you've fallen under a bus or decided to take unauthorized leave. I don't know why, but I covered for you today. I told Mr Thatcher you had a bug, which was believable since you've had time off recently. I only did it because you were such a mess yesterday, but just so you know, I will NOT do it again tomorrow. You'd better get in touch ASAP. If you don't you might not have a job to come back to.

Hazel
PS. If I don't hear from you, I will also call the police.

The only surprising part of her mail is that she covered for me. I'll call her and tell her I'm in a worse state than I let on, or that there was an emergency and I had to come back to Scotland. I rummage in my bag for the phone I switched off yesterday. It takes me right back to the last conversation I had on it. I take a deep breath, wipe my palms and turn the phone back on. It beeps to tell me I have a message. That will be Hazel. It beeps again. And again. And again, again, again. I look at the display that says I have 16 missed calls. I never have 16 calls in a week, let alone in a single day. Ever.

Fearful of what they might find, my fingers scroll slowly over the list of unsuccessful callers, which include Hazel, a number I don't recognise, an 'unknown', and my mother, who does not make a habit of phoning me on my mobile.

The first message is from the unknown caller, and whoever it is just hangs up without speaking. The next is my mother's number. She too says nothing, but I can hear her breathing. Then comes Hazel asking me where I am, followed by silence from a number I don't recognise, followed by several more hang-ups from the unknown caller. It goes on like that, and I think the only actual message is going to be from Hazel, until I hear James's voice saying he would really like to talk to me and find out how I am.

I don't need to look in a mirror to know I'm smiling. I listen to his message a second and even a third time. His voice is warm and friendly and allows me to think he might like me more than he let on in our hotel room in Scarborough. I should call him back.

My mother comes into the room.

"Hey mum, I see you tried to call me yesterday."

She walks over to the window, and is silent for a moment before she replies.

"Did I?"

"My phone says you did."

She turns to face me.

"…does it? That's clever…"

"Didn't you?"

"I don't remember."

"No?"

"Errm… oh yes… that's right. I think I did try you."

"Any special reason?"

"Do you know, I can't remember. Just to say hello, I think. Have you finished on the computer?"

"Almost."

"Did you find what you were looking for?"

"No."

"Well, dinner is almost ready."

She returns to the kitchen, leaving her memory loss behind. Its presence is heavy and makes me long for the woman I have spent years keeping at arm's length.

"I just need to write an email first. If that's all right…"

"Hurry up then."

I've decided to write to Hazel rather than phoning her. I know it's the coward's way out, but I don't want to incur her wrath voice-to-voice. I'm composing my reply in my head as I scan through the rest of the messages in my email in-box. Besides the work stuff, which I'm not going to look at now, it's all spam; people asking me to lend them money, or trying to sell me medicines to enlarge anatomical features I don't even have. I systematically delete them, and am almost finished when I get to one that catches my eye.

To: RMorton@BaldNoMore.co.uk
From: Info@BicycleBooks.co.uk
Subject: Walden

Hello Ruth
I hope you got back home safely. It was really nice to meet you up here and it's a shame you had to leave so soon. I've been trying to call you. No luck so far, so hoping this will reach you. It's about Walden's book, which I know from someone called Magdalena Borkowski (interesting story) you left in the Grand. If you have a moment, we should talk about it. I'm not sure Walden is of sound mind. Even less so than I first thought.

Call me.
James

What on earth…
"Ruth, dinner!"
My stomach has turned on the idea of food. Who is Magdalena Borkowski? And what does he know that I don't?
"Ruth!"
How does he know more than me?
"Are you coming? It'll go cold."
The table is set like it always is, so we will eat facing one another across its width rather than its length. The sight of it and the smell of shepherd's pie take me back to so many nights of my life, to awkward quiet and the sense that she and I were never really meant to be.
I sit. She puts the pie on the table and takes her place.
"Dig in, then."
"Thanks, it looks great."
She puts a big dollop on my plate and stares at me.
"Which is more than I can say for you. Was everything all right with your email?"
"Yes."

"No bad news of any kind?"

"No."

"Are you sure?"

I try to look sure.

"Certain."

"No man trouble then?"

"No man troubles."

I flash her a look I hope tells her to move onto a different subject.

"Go on then, eat your pie."

"I'm not hungry."

"I thought you said you were starving."

"I was. But I'm actually not feeling all that well."

"In what way?"

"Just a bit sick."

"Aye, well you're probably over hungry. All you need's a good meal."

I eat, knowing that what I need is to understand what Magdalena Boro-thingy has read to prompt her to get in touch with Dragonfly Press and ultimately with me. I have to speak to James and get him to get my book back so I can clear his name.

"It's delicious, mum, but I don't think I can eat anymore."

"You've barely touched it."

"I have."

"I've known flies eat more than that."

"I'm sorry. Perhaps I'll finish it up later. I'm feeling a bit faint. Do you mind if I go and get some fresh air."

"Faint now as well?"

"A little."

"Like I said, you need feeding up."

"It's nothing a breath of air won't fix."

"Well I'm not going to sit here and force feed you. If you need fresh air, you'd better go and get some. Will you be long?"

"No."

"I'll put the kettle on and we can have a nice cup of tea when you get back."

- 42 -

By the time she dished up the shepherd's pie, Morna Morton was feeling severely tested. Ruth was driving her to distraction. Not only did she doggedly refuse to admit to having a boyfriend, but she thought her too old or too stupid to have a computer. Even Jenny Better had one now and she was much older and more stupid.

Then there was the pie itself. It might not have been up to London standards, but Morna had gone to quite some trouble to make it. Rather than settling on a packet of minced beef, she'd ground some lamb trimmings and mashed her potatoes with top of the milk to get a beautiful creamy texture. It was one of her signature dishes, and she could make it with her eyes closed. But on the occasion of her daughter's unexpected return, she kept them open and tried her very best to make it a meal to match any of the fancy stuff on offer in England.

While Ruth had tended to whatever internet business had suddenly been so pressing, Morna had laid the table with her best plates and some lovely new napkins she'd bought in honour of her last visitor from London. She'd hoped her daughter would appreciate the little details, but when, after being summoned three times, she had finally come to the table, she'd said nothing about how nice everything looked, and had sat down and poked at the food before declaring she was not hungry and needed fresh air.

Fresh air. Those were the words that alerted Morna to what was really going on. As she cleared the table in preparation of the cup of tea she'd promised Ruth on her return, she thought back thirty plus years to her own loss of appetite, her fatigue, her faintness, and the nausea which she'd only ever been able to still with a walk in the fresh air.

Although she could not say for sure whether Ruth already understood her predicament, Morna was quite certain that her daughter was carrying a child.

- 4 3 -

James Hunter was sitting in his office nearing the end of Walden's book when he finally received the call he'd been waiting for. He felt his heart skip a proverbial beat when Ruth's voice drifted down the line, and had to concentrate as hard to keep the thud out of his voice as he did to remind himself it was his duty to share with her his worst suspicions.

He pictured her standing in a busy London side street - the type he would have spent time in had he ever fulfilled his journalistic ambitions - having snatched a moment to fit in a brief call to himself. That being so, he didn't have long to capture and keep her attention. His delivery needed to be spot on, well-paced and concerned.

"It's good to hear from you. How have you been?"

"Fine, thank you."

"Good. That's excellent."

"And you?"

"Mustn't grumble, as they say round my way, but then do anyway."

She offered him a polite laugh that made him cringe at his own lame attempt at humour.

"I've been trying to call you."

"I know. I got your message. And your mail."

"I'm glad you called back."

"You asked me to."

In his rehearsed version of this conversation, she hadn't made him work quite so hard.

"I did, you're quite right. I just thought it, errm, I just thought it would be nice to say hello and see how you are-doing, because I really enjoyed meeting you the other night. And you know, if you ever fancy popping up again sometime, I'd be happy to show you the Scarborough sights. Penny machines, donkeys on the beach, fish and chips fresh from the sea, the fish at least... oh, and we have an excellent super loo on the prom."

"You paint a vivid picture."

This time her laugh sounded more genuine, and it gave him the nudge he needed.

"Always flying the flag for Scarborough... What about you anyway? How's London?"

"I'm not in London."

"No? I thought you said you worked there."

"I'm taking a couple of days off. Again."

"Are you coming back up to Scarborough? It really is a superb super-loo."

"I'm in Scotland visiting my mum."

"Scotland? Whereabouts?"

"On Iona."

He hadn't been prepared for that.

"Iona, huh?"

"It's an island. Really small, but very pretty. I'm looking at the sea."

"And you're there right now?"

"Yes. A safe distance from Walden and his book."

It was his cue, but his nerves kept him from taking it.

"At least I thought it was."

"Yeah, I'm sorry to drag him into your holiday."

"That's not what I meant."

He was sweating.

"I don't know if you saw my mail. Probably seems like I'm the stalker now, phone calls and emails. Thing is, I got a mail from someone called Magdalena Borkowski."

"I know. I read your mail."

"You did? Good. You need to be more careful with your books."

"I left it here on purpose. Now I wish I hadn't. What did she say, this Magdalena?"

"She was in a right old flap, asking me how I could publish something so unsettling. I was going to write back and tell her I didn't, but that would have opened a can of worms I can't close, so...."

"So...?"

"So I wrote to you instead."

"Can you get her to send it to you? So much has happened in the past 48 hours. I have the growing sense that if I want find out what Walden wants, I'm going to have to finish reading it."

He weighs up his options. Then goes for broke.

"I... I have a copy of it."

Not the gentle approach he'd intended.

"Of the book?"

"Yes."

"But... but how? You said there was only one."

"I photocopied it when you left it in my office."

"What? The whole thing?"

"I know it was a tad cheeky but, to be honest, I was so pissed off that someone had been using my company's name without checking in with me first, that I wanted to find out what it was all about. I thought it might be someone with a grudge against me."

He didn't know her well enough to interpret the silence on the line.

"Are you mad? I'd get it if you were. I probably would be.'

"Do you still think that... about the grudge?"

"No."

"So you don't think it has anything to do with you?"

"Not really... Hey, I'm sorry. I should have asked."

"Have you read it?"

"Most of it."

"And is this Magdalena woman right about it being unsettling?"

There was no easy way to tell her what Magdalena Borkowski had really said.

"Is she?"

"I'm not sure. But I have to ask you something, and I don't want you to take it the wrong way because it's not me prying into your personal life."

Knowing there was more riding on her answer than her vulnerability to Walden's insanity, he took a deep breath and braced himself for the worst.

- 4 4 -

Morna set the cups on the table and scalded the pot in preparation for the tea. Not too strong, not too sweet. She sat
down thinking of the little baby growing in her daughter's
belly and felt the same surge of warmth she had experi-
enced the morning after she dreamed of becoming a
grandmother.

She still felt a niggle that she'd not yet met the father-
to-be nor, for that matter, even heard Ruth volunteer his
name, but decided to believe there must be a good reason
for that. A logical one would be Tod Walden's age. It
wouldn't be easy for a man at his time of life to welcome a
new baby into the world. The more she thought about it, the
more she convinced herself that her daughter was in fact
aware of her pregnancy, had met with resistance from her
partner, and come to Iona to escape his insistence that she
get rid of the child.

This sequence of events equipped Morna with great understanding, for nobody knew better than she about the
importance of finding a safe place for a baby. She only
wished Ruth would confide in her and ask for the help she
would bend and fall over herself to provide. It would be her
way of making amends. Whatever she had failed to do as a
mother, she would do double from her place one branch
higher in the family tree.

Thinking of the mother-to-be, Morna realised she was
growing slightly anxious at her prolonged absence. She
went into the front room where she had a better view over
the island, but Ruth was nowhere within sight. She considered going out after her to make sure she was alright, but

reminded herself she must be measured in her behaviour if she didn't want to give herself away.

To pass the time while she waited for Ruth's return, she went to her computer to block the next three weeks from prospective B&B guests. When she touched the keyboard to call the computer back to life, she was not greeted with the Highlands scenery that the computer man had installed for her, but by an email addressed to Ruth.

Had it not been for the fact that her eyes picked up the name "Walden" in the subject line of the message, Morna would almost certainly have walked away again without reading it. But as it was, she felt it her right as the future grandmother of the man's child to know a little bit about him.

- 4 5 -

He is waiting, and he is tired of so doing. He feels as if he has been waiting half of his life, and considers calling it a day, marching over to her house, making himself a cup of tea, taking a place in one of her armchairs, and waiting for her to return. He could easily do all of that. But he won't.

He won't because he believes in sticking to a plan, especially a plan he spent so long forging and honing, and one which he committed to the paper he still firmly believes she has on her person wherever the devil she is.

He has phoned her many times, but not once has she answered, which leads him to believe that the phoney census reviewer might have had, and therefore given him, the wrong number. He was not raised in an environment that gladly suffered the likes of fools, and does not like to be made to look like one now, *Foxtrot to the lavatory backwards? What an idiot! (4)*.

He hopes the man responsible will put in another appearance at her front door, and vows to show no mercy if the occasion should arise. Who would be the bonehead then, *Takes a numbskull to heed a good French word! (8)*?

He would contact her fat colleague, whose name he happens to know is Hazel, if it were still office hours. He will do so in the morning if she has not returned by then, and will say he is calling from her insurance company and must speak to her on a matter of some importance. He will not take no for an answer and, if fat Hazel refuses to divulge her whereabouts, he will say her house has been broken into. She has idiocy, *Just stupidity to think half diode would work in such a cold state (6)*, written all over her, so he is certain she will fall for what will not, strictly speaking, be a lie.

- 4 6 -

"Do I have a boyfriend? That's your question?"

"I told you it would sound nosey."

It does. It also sends a little bolt of excitement through me.

"You don't have to answer. It's just that in Walden's book Davina has a boyfriend, or a "lover" as he calls it, who turns out to be married, except Davina doesn't seem to know he's married until Tod Walden knocks on the door of the lover's wife."

This is not good.

"Walden seems to think the lover is called Thor, although Davina says his name is Paul. Does any of that chime with you?"

I feel as if someone has punched me square in the stomach. I have to sit down. No, I have to walk. I have to speak to him. But I don't know what to say. I can hear him breathing, and that is comforting, however many miles away he is. I have to talk to him, say something, anything before he takes his breath away from my ear.

"Ruth? Are you still there?"

"Yes."

"Are you okay?"

"His real name is Paul. Not Thor. And Walden is right, I didn't know he was married."

"So there is a Thor character in your real life?"

"There was. Until a couple of days ago."

"What happened to him?"

"Exactly what you just said."

"Woah… seriously? How fucked up is that?"

I can't talk. What can I say when I understand nothing myself? If I didn't know he was married, how did Walden? How? Who the hell is he? And what does he want from me?

"Ruth?"

When I first sat down on this bench outside the Abbey, it felt like a safe and familiar place, but now, with the sun all but drained out of the sky, Walden is lurking in the shadows.

"Ruth? Are you still there?"

I nod.

"Ruth?"

"Yes."

"Are you okay?"

"No. I'm scared."

"I get that. I'd be scared too if someone had singled me out, stalked me, written a book for me and is... I don't suppose this is helping much, is it?"

"I don't get it. Any of it. And you know what else? My mother reckons she read an article or a review about him."

"About Walden? Where?"

"I don't know. She's getting older and more forgetful, and says she can't remember."

"Did she say what it was about? Did it mention the book?"

"She doesn't know. She just said it was about a book he wrote. But that's strange too, because it could mean he's written more than one. But I can't find any mention of him as a writer anywhere."

"Can't she remember anything specific?"

"Only that he's a writer and he's in a relationship with a Scottish woman." As I say the last two words, their impact meets me full on. I don't know how I managed to dodge them when my mother spoke them earlier, but there's no escape now.

"Oh my God, he might mean me."

James is quiet.

"What am I going to do?"

"You're going to read the rest of the book, which I'll get to you, and we're going to work out who Walden is and what he wants from you. And in the meantime, take great care of yourself and your mother."

"My mother?"

"I don't want to scare you any more than I already have, but I think he's probably capable of more than just breaking up a relationship."

"What has that got to do with my mother?"

"Davina's mother is mentioned in the book. And so is Iona."

"Iona the place? It's a name as well, you know."

"Not in Walden's book."

"What does it say?"

- 47 -

Shelagh Law went out as the victim of a strange twist of fate which bore the hallmark of a practical joke from on high. Just days after being reunited with Tod, the love of her life, she delighted at his suggestion that they take to the waters near her home in order to catch that evening's dinner.

Had she known, Dear Reader, how the years had eaten away at his muscles and his hearing, she might not have been so hasty. But as it was, she had been without him for too long to pass up the opportunity of what she assured herself would be a wonderful afternoon spent bobbing about in the coastal waters of the North Atlantic.

It might have been just that, had destiny not intervened and hooked a large fish on the end of Tod's line. As he stood in the rocky rowing boat trying to tame the creature that thrashed about in a wild attempt to secure its right to life, she had visions of their return to shore. They would hold their giant catch above their heads and be hailed as the day's heroes by the villagers who, led by Davina, would gather in excitement around the happy new couple and their scaly evening meal. So lost was the old woman in this particular reverie that she failed to notice the wave that was virtually upon them. And before she could react to its advent, it had knocked Tod off balance and hurled him, rod and all, into the swirl it left in its angry wake.

It would have been a watery end for poor Tod were it not for Shelagh who, within seconds of realising the danger afoot, had jumped into the surf and taken hold of him. As she dragged her panic-stricken booty through the salty water towards their boat, smiling now at the thought of her life-

saver's welcome on shore, she was unaware of the fishing line becoming wrapped around her legs.

Deep below the surface, the fish on the end of Tod's line was swimming in frantic circles as it tried to free itself from the skewer in its bottom lip. Although it did not achieve its goal, it did manage to catch its catcher's lover.

Shelagh was almost at the edge of the boat when she was dragged under the first time. She let go of Tod who, still clutching his rod, was able to climb back into their little vessel. As he did so, she disappeared beneath the surface again, emerging in a state of panic a few moments later. Understanding that the fish was still attached to his line and that the same line was now attached to her, she shouted at him to cut her free. But her pleas, Dear Reader, failed to reach his ears, which were clogged with old age, salt water, and perhaps a hint of revenge, so that by the time the sun set over Iona that same evening, the rescued man was fully re-covered, while Shelagh lay dead in her front room.

- 4 8 -

"Shall I keep reading?"

"No. No more."

Somewhere in Scarborough - in my mind it is the room at the Grand Hotel - James is standing holding a pile of photocopied pages. He is sharing their contents with a woman sitting on a bench outside the abbey on the island which features in the story he has read to her. Like everything about *The Ruthlessness of One Man*, it seems impossible, but I know enough by now to understand that Walden has followed me home.

"Who is Shelagh?"

The length and breadth of the ensuing moments are filled with the silence of his steeling himself. I know exactly what's coming next.

"She's Davina's mother. There's a reference on the next page."

And I am right.

"You mean my mother?"

"We don't know that for sure…"

I know he's trying to let me down gently, and I'm dimly appreciative, but there is no soft landing for such information. It falls like the stones of the walls against which I sit. My thoughts are moving slowly, too slowly, to become clear. As they crawl themselves towards a clearing in my mind, all I know is that my mother has no place in Walden's book. He can have me if he really has to, but he's not having her.

"…Shelagh could be purely fictional."

"That's not likely though is it, not in light of Paul."

The cold of the old abbey building has slipped inside me. It's time to go home. I get up to leave, but retreat to the bench when I notice a man by the gate at the top of the slope. I lean against the wall as hard as I can, willing the saints I am told have been here, to absorb me from his view.

"Probably not. Do your parents live on Iona?"

"My mother does."

I have my eye on the dusky outline of the man. He's coming towards me, his every step pushing my heart a little further towards to my mouth.

"What's her name?"

"Ssshhhh."

"Ruth?"

The man is now only a few yards away and even through the gathering darkness I can tell he's looking directly at me. Fear is tugging at me to leave, but to get back to the road I'd have to pass him or walk around the back of the Abbey, which would put me out of sight of the road, and that is not a chance I'm willing to take.

"There's a man… he's coming towards me."

"I can't hear you. You've gone very quiet."

"There's a man heading straight for me."

And so he is. I move the phone from my ear, but keep it turned on. I want James to hear whatever comes next.

"Good evening."

It's him. I can tell by the way he's looking at me that it's him. It must be.

"You got a light?"

It takes me a second to realise what he means and, when I do, my relief chokes me.

"My damn lighter's empty."

"I don't smoke."

"You and the rest of the country. Can't get a light for love nor money these days."

As he starts out back up the slope, taking his unlit cigarette with him, I return to James.

"Sorry. It's getting really dark here. Too many shadows."

I get up and start walking back to my mother's house.

"Ruth? Do you have any idea at all who Walden might be?"

"Don't you think I'd have mentioned that by now?"

"Fair point. But do you think he might be someone you know? Someone with a score to settle?"

"I don't have any open scores."

My answer is a reaction, but I really don't. I don't have any enemies.

"What about your married man?"

"He's not mine. But what about him?"

"I suppose he'd be unlikely to shop himself... Forget I said that. Could it be someone in your family?"

"My family is tiny; just me, my mum, my aunt, and a couple of cousins. And why would they put me through this?"

"I wish I knew."

Neither of us speaks for a moment, and the silence swells with our respective thoughts.

"What about your mum, do you think she might know Walden? Could there be someone on the island looking for revenge?"

"Revenge for what?"

"I don't know."

"People on this island are good..."

"There are always exceptions."

"Not here, there aren't. And anyway, if it was a local, how would they know about my life in England?"

"I honestly don't know. But I want to find out... Here's a thought... actually no, that doesn't make sense either."

"What?"

"It's nothing."

"Go on, tell me."

"I was just going to say... have you considered the possibility that Walden might be your mother?"

"No. She wouldn't. She couldn't. Why would she?"

"I don't know. I don't know your mother."

As I think about the absurdity of this suggestion, a charge of possibility surges through me. "...maybe you're right. Maybe she is involved somehow. That could explain her mentioning an article about Walden."

"It could. But it might not."

"She's my mother. She wouldn't do this to me."

"Just read the rest of the book. I'll send you my photocopied pages tomorrow… Or I could bring them to you."

"Where?"

"To wherever you are."

"To Iona?"

"Why not?"

An ember of excitement glows inside me.

"It's a long way away, and complicated to reach. You have to get boats and buses and trains…"

"I'm from Scarborough, we're used to getting around on donkeys, so I'm sure I can cope with a bit of public transport."

I'm not sure what to say. I'm a few metres from my mother's door now, and the sight of the light on in the living room brings me back to reality. Having him here would give rise to a string of questions I wouldn't be able to answer even if I wanted to.

"Sleep on it and let me know. If you don't want me to come, I'll get my photocopy to the post first thing."

"I'll think about it."

"And in the meantime, I'd play it safe for a while if I were you."

"How do you mean?"

"Just take care."

I can't recall the last time someone told me to take care. Two tiny words, spoken with warmth. I want to nestle into them and stay there.

- 49 -

Morna read the email from this James several times before finally closing it and setting about the business that had taken her to her computer in the first place. But she could not get the words "I'm not sure Walden is of sound mind" out of her own.

She concluded, more because she wanted to than because she had hard evidence to back her up, that her daughter must somehow be involved in the promotion of her boyfriend's books, and that this James was trying to come between them. She had no ready explanation for anyone called Magdalena something or other, but that seemed of secondary importance. What mattered was Ruth's well-being. Emotional and physical.

She therefore decided to mention nothing about what she had read, but to bide her time until her daughter's pregnancy forced her into a corner from which she would divulge everything Morna wanted to know. But as she sat in her own corner waiting for Ruth to come home from her breath of fresh air, she had to summon her powers of denial to fight off thoughts that Tod Walden might be as deranged as the email suggested.

Within a matter of a very few minutes, that question mark drove Morna to the phone. The investigator picked up on the second ring and seemed to slur a little as he spoke. But drunk or not drunk, Morna had nobody else she could call on to go and find out everything they could about the father of her grandchild.

- 5 0 -

James held the phone in his hand for several minutes after the line went dead, trying to decide whether she had led him to believe he was welcome or unwelcome on her island. He considered phoning Ruth back to clarify, but after lifting and replacing the handset more times than he felt fitting for a man of his age, he opted to tough it out and wait for her to let him know what she wanted him to do. He had extended his offer, and anything more than that would be too much.

Although he knew his decision to be the right one, that didn't make it an easy companion, and for the first 45 minutes following their conversation, he simmered in anticipation of a return call. When it failed to materialise, he gave himself two options. The first was to knuckle down and do the right thing by his customers, the second, to head along the promenade to his local to do the wrong thing by himself. He tossed for it, tossed again, then picked up the remaining photocopies from Walden's book, telling himself he would finish it first, then do some work, then reward himself with a swift half.

However, upon reaching the end of *The Ruthlessness of One Man* half an hour later, he was in possession of a new, unequivocal plan. He had been wrong to suggest Ruth's mother might have written the book, but he had not been wrong about everything. Now almost certain that the writer and his protagonist were no strangers to each other, he was convinced that Ruth's world was about to turn on its axis, and that it would claim casualties as it went.

There was no indication as to exactly when this might happen, which meant he had to act fast. His internet search for Iona proved to James it was about time he sat down to dinner with a map. He was surprised to learn that it would take him at least eight hours to reach the tiny dot off the south west coast of Mull, and that was without the time he was likely to have to spend waiting for not one, but two ferries. If it meant, however, that he could protect Ruth from a madman who believed she was his right, it was a journey he would have made seven times over.

- 51 -

He has just woken from a five-minute nap when he sees someone at her front door. It is too dark for him to make out who it is, but he is certain from the height of the figure it is not her. He hurries out of his own house, feeling for the key to hers as he goes, and smiles when he sees the phoney census officer rapping at her door. If he is not mistaken, the man is swaying slightly, which he hopes means he is under the influence, *Beguiled, besotted or just below the table? (5, 3, 9)*, as smashed, *Destroyed potato within, but in Latin! (7)*, he will be easier to deal with.

His suspicion is confirmed when the man opens his mouth and unleashes into the night a savage smell of stale scotch, *Spirit found in child's bed in south Switzerland (6)*. He smiles and offers his adversary a greeting of genuine welcome.

He does as he did the last time and opens her door for the man who has come looking for her, but who is too drunk this time to keep up the pretence of having been sent by a government office that is blind to his pathetic existence. Once again they go into the kitchen where he offers the man a drink from the bottle of cheap single malt he knows she keeps in the third cupboard left of her cooker. He accepts because he is equally cheap, and a drunkard to boot, *Confused Kurd ran after dog initially – he's the worse for wear (8)*.

The man takes the drink and a first step towards coming clean about his real reasons for being there. He says he has nothing to do with any census review but is a private investigator, hired by an old Scottish woman who wants him to pry into her daughter's affairs.

He listens with interest and presses the private eye for more information. With a boozy chortle and air of abandon, the man confesses that this time round, on his client's instruction, it is he, Tod Walden, who is the subject of his investigation.

He is quietly enraged by this search for information to which the Scottish biddy has neither a right nor a hope of receiving. He tops up the stranger's glass and takes advantage of his inebriation to ascertain one or two facts for himself. As the detective has no respect for anything but the colour of money, it is easy work.

He is quickly able to confirm the old bag in question goes by the name Morna Morton. It is not news to him, because he has done his research well and knows that she lives in a white house, a B&B uninspiringly called Sea View, next to the only post office on the island of Iona. He did not, however, know that it had a green front door, because the photographs he has seen on his various expeditions through the albums in the next room show it to be red. He was equally unaware that the battle-axe "makes a decent pot of porridge", is good for a "nice drop of scotch", but is "a bit stiff around the elbow" and currently has no vacancies in her two-up, two-down because her daughter Ruth is visiting.

He cannot hide the anger which grips him upon hearing this last piece of information and notes the stranger watching him with interest as he bangs first one then both fists on the table. She was supposed to return to the island with him. They were supposed to drive there together. Did he not make that plain enough? Or is she intentionally set on vexing him?

He takes a deep breath and tells himself that she would not have gone to Iona of her own volition, but must have been coerced there by her scheming mother. He is overcome with a spasm of wrath strong enough to pull him up out of his chair and knock the investigator, who is the closest thing to the hag, out of his. The man is too drunk to know what is happening and is easy prey for the fury that has been building in him for the past two days and which now finds its way to the surface through his hands and feet.

He kicks and hits and kicks the body on the floor for as long as it takes his ire and his breath to run out. When he is done, he does not check for a pulse, but smoothes his grey hair and suit and lets himself out into the night through the back door.

I'm kicking myself for not taking James up on his offer to come. Mother or no mother.

"Ru-uth?"

Think of the devil...

"Ru-uuthy... Oh *there* you are."

I walk up the path to where she's standing in her slippers waving a torch and looking both like and unlike the mother I know.

"Thank heavens. Where have you been? I've been worried sick."

"I was just having a walk."

"You've been gone getting on for two hours. It won't do for you to be standing out here. Come in before you perish."

She puts her arm tightly around my waist and guides me inside as if I were blind. Her hand rubs the same spot on my side over and over again. There is something manic in the movement and I want to pull free of her and whatever dead brain cells are making her behave in this way. She ushers me inside and steers me towards the kitchen table set with teacups. Without saying a word, she pushes me into one of the chairs and goes to the stove to fill the pot.

"One sugar or two? I always used to like it with two when...'

"Actually mum, I think I could do with something a bit stronger."

"We can leave it to brew for a few minutes. It'll be strong enough."

"No, I don't mean strong tea."

"What then?"

"Whisky?"

"Whisky?"

"Yes, do you have any?"

"I do… but are you sure you want it?"

"Yes."

"It's not good for you. Not in your…"

"I only want a drop."

"It's cheap stuff. I don't think you'd like it."

"I'm not fussed. I could just do with something to warm me."

"Aye, and that's why I'm standing here making tea."

I feel like we're singing *There's a hole in my bucket, dear Liza, dear Liza…* But I really don't want a cup of tea. I get up and go to the Welsh dresser.

"Is it in here?"

She nods, her face crumpled with disapproval.

"I'll just have a mouthful and then a cup of tea. Okay?"

She doesn't reply.

"Do you want one?"

"No."

"It doesn't look too cheap to me. This is the good stuff."

She brings the tea, I, the bottle and a glass. We sit, neither of us saying anything. I recognise this mood, this distance established to punish my crime of disobedience. But it's the least of my worries tonight. The question I can't get out of my head is whether she has something to do with Walden's book. It is on my tongue, working its way to the tip.

"It's still not right for someone in your state."

I am not sure what state she is referring to. I'm either not doing as good a job of keeping my worries to myself as I thought, or I was right to think she's losing her mind.

"What do you mean?"

She looks at me just long enough to show she's hiding something.

"Mum?"

"Oh, I've just remembered I forgot to change the reservation status of the house. How long did you say you'd be staying?"

"I don't know. It depends."

"On what?"

"On you. Among other things."

"I don't mind how long you stay. No need to rush away like you usually do."

She's hovering in the doorway, but not looking at me.

"I'll say we're closed for bookings for the next two weeks. Will that do to start with?"

I don't know if it's the effect of the whisky I'm sipping, or the homeliness of the fire leaping in the grate in front of me, but two weeks doesn't seem like enough.

"Can we make it three?"

Now she turns. And she smiles.

"Of course."

She goes through to the front room, and I let my thoughts drift towards Scarborough, to where I imagine James in his office. I hear his suggestion to come and see me here, at my mother's house. I reach for the whisky bottle and pour another small glass, which I raise to him and me.

"That's that taken care of."

My mother is talking as she comes back to the kitchen.

"You have your room for the next three weeks. Except for tomorrow night, I'm afraid. A booking has come in for that and the system won't allow me to cancel."

She sits down opposite me, blocking my view of the fire, removes my whisky glass, pours me some tea, and smiles like she so rarely does.

- 53 -

Back at the table with her daughter, Morna was verging on happy. Not only had Ruth actually come right out and asked if she could stay for as many as three weeks, which would be the longest period of time she had spent at home for years, but tomorrow they would be receiving a visit from none other than Mr Tod Walden, as the name on the online booking form had said.

Morna was tempted to share the good news but decided that if this Mr Walden wanted Ruth to know he was coming, he would have told her himself. And the fact that he hadn't made her think it must be a surprise. She would therefore simply play dumb and watch the reunion as it happened. In the meantime, however, it couldn't do any harm to push her daughter a little more for the real reason behind her unannounced arrival on Iona.

"Oh, I'm sorry, but I had to close your email when I was checking the bookings."

"I didn't know it was open."

"Aye it was. Something about a book."

"You read my email?"

"No, no. I just happened to notice the word book, that's all. I hope I didn't delete anything when I closed it."

"It wouldn't matter if you did."

"Oh... so it wasn't an important message then?"

"No."

Morna knew if she wanted to move onto another level with her daughter, this was a moment she had to seize.

"And I could have sworn I saw the name Walden as well."

"I thought you said you didn't read it?"

"I didn't."

"But you saw the name Walden?"

"I thought I did. But I might be wrong. It might be my old age. I seem to misread things a lot at first glance. I get them muddled up with things I'm thinking about, and after our conversation about Mr Walden, it might just be that..."

Morna was watching her daughter carefully as she spoke, scanning her features for any hint of a reaction which could be a hint itself. And she might have congratulated herself for her attention to detail were it not for the fact that what she saw was an expression so filled with fear that it ignited her own.

"Okay mum, what do you know about Walden?"

"Nothing."

"I don't believe you. You keep talking about him, so just tell me what you know. I mean it. You have to tell me."

Ruth was on her feet, making Morna feel small in more ways than one, and too small by far to reveal the identity of her source.

"I... I don't know what you're talking about. Maybe I didn't see his name. Betty says she reads things wrongly too."

"I don't care what Betty says. That's not the point. I want to know why you keep talking about this Mr Walden."

"I don't."

"Yes you do, and now you have to explain. Do you know him?"

Morna was genuinely puzzled.

"Of course I don't know him. How on earth could I know him?"

"You tell me."

"Ruth, you should calm down. It's not good for you to get too excited."

"I'm not excited. I'm just asking you a question, and I want you to answer me honestly."

"I have. I don't know him."

"In that case, why are you so fascinated by him?"

"I do wish you'd come and sit down. Your pacing is making me nervous."

"I don't want to sit down. What's your fascination with Walden?"

"I think you're getting mixed up, dear. I was just saying I thought I saw his name on your email, which seemed like a coincidence after we talked about him. That's all."

"That's all?"

"What more should there be?"

"I don't know."

"Well then… Unless there is anything you want to tell me?"

Morna could see her daughter's thoughts shift in a different direction and for one hopeful second, she thought Ruth was going to reveal what she wanted to hear.

"No. Nothing."

"Are you sure?"

"Certain. Let's just drop it. No more talk of Mr Walden."

"If you say so."

Morna got up to move the teapot, more out of a need to consider her next move than anything else.

"Although I can't help but wonder why… he's just a writer, isn't he?"

"No he's not. He's a madman, and he doesn't care how his writing affects other people's lives. Including mine. And yours for that matter."

Ruth walked out of the kitchen, banging the door behind her in a way not even the wind knew how, and leaving Morna to the safety of her teapot and the knowledge that Mr Walden's impending arrival on the island was going to be challenging.

She sat in contemplation for a good half hour after Ruth's sudden departure, sketching out the possible scenarios that had led to it. Her preferred one was that Ruth had always played second fiddle to Walden's writing, but that now she was pregnant – and this theory assumed that both the mother and father-to-be did in fact know about the baby – she wanted to move up to first place. Walden, she mused, may well have set Ruth an ultimatum. Him or the infant.

That would explain Ruth's aggression and, she realised with a jolt of fear, why she had been so eager to reach for the whisky bottle.

Morna knew all about turning to hard liquor to terminate an unwanted pregnancy. She knew about sitting in cold and then scalding baths, and she knew about starvation, but she was not willing to stand by and let Ruth do any of that. She would have to keep a close eye on her. She would not ask questions, but she would give her anything and everything she could possibly need in order to underscore the value of motherhood.

She would go upstairs in a moment and take Ruth a hot water bottle and mug of cocoa, but she had a quick call to make beforehand.

She reached for the telephone and redialled the last number she had used. She wanted to know as much about this Mr Tod Walden as possible before he arrived on her doorstep in less than 24 hours.

- 54 -

I wake to feel my hot water bottle turned cold pressing against my toes. I push it away, remembering the image of my mother tucking it under my covers last night as it flops onto the carpet. The memory takes me back to the thoughts that were circling when sleep claimed me, to the question of my mother's involvement in Walden's book. Those thoughts are stirring with me, and they want an answer.

I open the curtains to an amazing blue sky. Its clarity floods the room, assuring me that my mother could have no reason to write herself to death in the waters which now glisten up at me with all the promise of that impossibility.

"Hello?"

I didn't hear her open the door.

"Good morning, dear. I thought you might like a wee breakfast. Nothing too heavy. Just a bowl of porridge and some tea."

"Oh, thanks mum. But I can come down and eat it."

"Nonsense."

She puts the tray on the chest of drawers, plumps my pillows like a nurse might, tightens the sheets, and ushers me back into bed.

"You just enjoy some quiet time. It'll do you good."

"But I never have breakfast in bed."

"You do today. Now go on, in you hop."

I climb in and let her pull the covers over me. Once there, she hands me the tray and tells me she'll come and collect it in a little while. I smile, vowing to get downstairs before she gets back up.

"Don't you need to get the room ready for the guest?"

"No hurry. I'm not expecting him until about five o'clock. And you'd better decide if you want to sleep in with me tonight or go on the sofa."

The times I've pictured my mother growing old, I've seen someone cantankerous and impossible to be with, not this fluffy woman who offers me a place in her bed and brings me breakfast in mine. She hadn't trained me for this and I'm not convinced I can become a different person just because she has.

"The sofa's fine."

"If you're sure. You can always change your mind later."

I eat the porridge and listen to the wild calls of the gulls. They lead me to Scarborough and to James, who has taken up near permanent residence in my mind. I replay his offer to visit me, and try to imagine us together here in this room. Maybe it's the sleep, or maybe it's the brightness of the day, but the picture doesn't look so wrong. Surely between us we could tackle my mother's inevitable questions. I finish eating and quickly get dressed. I'm going outside and, if I don't lose my nerve between now and the time I reach the beach at the back of the island, I'll call James to see if he is a man of his word.

- 5 5 -

Morna wasn't much surprised that the investigator failed to answer her calls. He'd slurred down the telephone in response to her request to find out more about Mr Walden, and she knew from his visit that he was a drinker. Nonetheless, she kept up her efforts to reach him. When Ruth went out to clear her mind, as she had put it, Morna pressed the redial button for the eighth time since getting up. But to no avail. She didn't leave a message because she didn't want him phoning the house and getting her daughter on the other end.

In the absence of any solid facts about Ruth's Mr Walden, Morna found it hard to like him, and unfairly easy to dislike him. She would reserve final judgement until he arrived at her door, but in the intervening hours she painted pictures of herself helping to raise the baby. The more she sat with the idea, the more she liked it. It would be her chance to make amends for her own mothering shortfalls. They might struggle for money a little, and she'd have to close her B&B to make space to accommodate them, but that wouldn't matter, because together they'd find a way to make ends meet.

When she went upstairs to prepare Ruth's room for Tod Walden, she found herself mentally rearranging it for his child. She would take one of the beds out and put a crib under the window, and maybe treat them to new wallpaper and curtains. She wasn't sure what would happen when the child became too big to share a room with its mother, but decided that was not a problem she had to solve immediately.

- 5 6 -

James was at a service station near the Scottish border when Ruth called him for the second time in as many days. He hadn't planned to speak to her again until he was closer to Iona, by which time, he figured, she'd be less likely to tell him to go back home. But when he saw her name on his phone, he didn't miss a beat in answering.

"Hello."

"Hey."

"This is Ruth."

"I know."

"Okay… well I was just calling to say I thought about what you said yesterday."

"Which bit of it?"

"All of it. Which is why I'm phoning. I can't really imagine that my mother wrote the book, or that she has anything to do with it. I can't work out what she knows or how, but I don't believe she actually knows Walden."

"Okay."

"I just wanted to tell you that."

"Well... thanks."

"You're welcome."

James was pleased that Ruth had phoned him to keep him up to date with her thoughts, but felt as if he were betraying her by not making it plain right there from his parking space, that even if Ruth's mother didn't know Walden, Walden seemed to think he knew her.

He wanted to tell her that after they'd finished speaking last night, he'd read the last pages of the book and that he now knew Tod was not only a name meaning sly, but the German word for dead. He wanted to shed the voyeuristic skin he felt he'd been forced into upon realising that *The Ruthlessness of One Man* had been written to reveal certain truths to its intended reader. But given the nature of those truths and the retribution he was now certain Walden was planning for the mother who had allegedly concealed them, he stood by his decision to tell Ruth face-to-face. Whether she wanted him to or not.

"Ruth, you know I said I could bring you the manuscript myself?"

"Yes?"

"Well, I am. I'm bringing it right now."

Had he practised telling her where he was and what he was en-route to do, he would have chosen a less frantic, less high-pitched tone. He would have encased his words in the casual manner that was usually his closest and unshakeable friend.

"Where to?"

"To Iona." When he spoke the name of her island to which he had not been invited, he almost felt as though he were trespassing.

"Really? You're coming here? Now?"

"Yes. A bit of sea air never did anyone any harm."

"But you live by the sea."

"Ah, but not on an island where I'd be surrounded by the stuff. At least not on a little island. And I thought I could combine my needs with yours. I know what the post is like, my book orders sometimes take days to reach customers. They love telling me all about that. And I thought you should have yours, your book that is, or photocopies of it, sooner rather than later. This way you'll have it tonight. What do you think?"

"I… I was just going to call you to say–"

"I know it's unexpected, and not what we agreed, but apart from anything else, I really would like to see you again."

"Oh… I…"

"And I won't get in your way, I promise. I've booked a hotel, and I can just come and drop the book off for you, then go again. If you want."

"No. You should have dinner with us. I'm sure my mother won't mind. If you call me when you're on the ferry from Mull to Iona...You do know you have to get two ferries, don't you?"

"I do."

"Well if you call me when you're on the second one, I'll come down to the pier to meet you."

"Sounds perfect."

"Do you have any idea what time it might be?"

"Probably not until early evening. I'm not actually in Scotland yet. Nearly at the border though."

"Then I guess I'll see you when you get here."

"I guess you will. I look forward to it." He hung up with the words "very much" bouncing on his tongue. Until he reminded himself that the reason for his visit was not strictly pleasure.

- 57 -

He loathes long journeys and, with every unit of distance he adds to the clock, he grows increasingly angry at having to travel the length of the country without her. Has she not finished his book, which clearly states they are to travel north together, and use the time involved in the tedious journey to talk through the finer points of how they will do away with the woman who so carelessly did away with him? He would have been happy to bludgeon her, *Imperial measure back to replace small fish's head at this bash (8)*, or better still to have her hung, drawn and quartered, *Distorted and wrung in hand before being billeted as severe punishment (4, 5, 3, 9)*. But they are messy ends, so he settled on a more gentle kind of murder, *Life draining event reversed about and after muddled percussion (6)*. Not that he sees it as anything other than a necessity.

He glances over into the back seat to make sure the fishing rods are still there and then returns his gaze to the road along which he travelled with futility many times and many years ago. The memory prods the anger that resides deep and complete within him, and he puts it to good use. He imagines wrapping his line around her mother's legs, and is in no doubt that he has what it takes to make it look like the accident it will certainly not be.

Appeased, he shifts his thoughts to life after that particular death – to life lived in truth. He looks forward to the praise he is certain she will lavish upon him when he reveals how he has been a regular visitor to her house since the day he noticed her sitting among a crowd of commuters. He will delight in explaining how he approached the elderly owner of the house opposite hers, and made him an offer he dared not refuse, and how he has been carefully and silently researching her life from that day forward. She will thank him for his ingenuity in turning the facts of her life into a book, and for the patience he has displayed in waiting for her to decipher the message from its pages.

He is most excited, however, at the prospect of telling her he will honour the destiny that brought her to him by never parting with her, and has their future together mapped out in a place far more isolated than the island towards which he is now travelling as fast as he possibly can.

- 5 8 -

"A friend? That's nice. I can't remember the last time you brought a friend home."

"I'm not bringing him home, he's coming to visit."

"He?"

"Yes."

"And how long does this 'he friend' of yours plan to stay?"

"Not long."

"How long is not long?"

"A day or two, I imagine. But you needn't worry, he's not going to stay with us."

"Is he not?"

"No. He's booked a room at the hotel."

"Are you sure?"

"Yes."

"But…?"

"But what?"

"Nothing, I just thought… why isn't he staying here? Did you tell him he could? If you really want to, the two of you can have my room and I'll go on the sofa."

I look at her waiting for a jack-in-the-box laugh to erupt, or at the very least an expression of embarrassment, but she offers neither. It's as though I've missed an episode in our lives, the one in which I tell her the kind of things that lead to her presumptuously suggesting I share her bed with a man I've only met once, and she never at all.

"I think it would be better if he stayed at the hotel."

"Suit yourself."

Her disapproval has crept back into the room, sweeping us high onto safe ground.

"Is he at least going to eat with us, your mystery friend?"

"Yes. And he isn't a mystery friend. His name is James and he comes from Yorkshire."

"James?"

"Yes."

"Oh. That's a nice name… And is that what people call him?"

Her question sounds as confused as she looks, and it worries me. I don't know how to handle this situation. Do I tell her I'm concerned about the state of her mind, or do I just watch and wait and see how things develop?

"Yes mum, that's what people call him."

She moves over to the sink to fill the kettle, which does not need to be boiled. I've seen her do it hundreds of times when contemplating what to say next.

"Nothing else? He doesn't have a nickname?"

"Some people call him Jim, but we can stick to James."

"Fine… And are you an item?"

"Mu-um."

"I'm only asking."

And I'm not telling.

"Well, how long have you known him? If I'm allowed to ask that."

"Not long."

"You and your not-longs. You should be glad I'm interested in your life and the people in it. What does he do for a living?"

"He's in the book business."

"Uh-huh?"

"Uh-huh."

"And is there anything else? Anything special I ought to know about him before he gets here? Anything you think might be of interest to me?"

"No."

I don't tell her about my excitement at the thought of seeing him again, or how I've been thinking about the way he held my face when he was on top of me in Scarborough and wondering if it will happen again. Neither do I let on that however little I know about him, I feel a sense of promise whenever he pops into my mind. And I certainly don't tell her what brought us together in the first place.

"Nothing you think he would want me to know about him? I wouldn't want to go putting my foot in any delicate situations."

"You won't."

The first thing I have to do when he gets here is tell him not to mention Walden to her. I don't want her to get any more involved than she is on paper.

- 59 -

Morna was more than a little puzzled by the sudden announcement that they were to be joined by someone called James, about whom Ruth was being deliberately and characteristically cagey. Her imagination served up three scenarios: one which saw her daughter in doubt as to the identity of the father of her unborn child, one in which she knew the father to be James but wished it were not, and one in which she knew it to be Walden but wished it were James.

Whichever was the case, she had the feeling that her daughter was not greatly looking forward to seeing her visitor. She, on the other hand, was. Since the breakdown in communications with the investigator, who resolutely refused to answer her calls, the imminent arrival of not one but two participants in Ruth's life was a godsend. Quite literally, and she felt certain it was by way of a reward for the restraint she had mustered in the past days.

Truth be told, she would have preferred to have both James and Tod Walden stay under her roof where she could keep a better eye on the two of them, but her house only had so many rooms, and not enough for that. So she would just have to make do with their company at dinner. She would do all she could to keep them both at her table for as long as possible, which would allow her to gain a greater sense of what was going on between the three of them.

She would serve them a meal from which they would not be in a hurry to get away and would engage them in the kind of conversations that allowed her to assess which one would make the better father, regardless of which one actually was.

When she went out to the garden to pick the herbs for her sage roast chicken, she glanced over to the Abbey, which looked magnificent against the pale blue sky. Quite without warning, she was transported inside to the baptismal font, and to a tiny baby boy in her daughter's arms.

It might have been the wind, emotion, or anticipation at the task awaiting her, but when she went back inside to chop the onions, there was a tear running down her cheek.

- 6 0 -

James had spent a week in the Scottish borders once and, although he thought the area perfectly nice, it had been a bit too neat for his taste and hadn't left him craving a repeat visit. Whenever the Scots he met on his travels around Scarborough thereafter raved about the beauty of their home turf, he told them he'd been there, seen it, and didn't understand what all the fuss was about. But on his drive from Glasgow to Oban, he was willing to admit he'd been too harsh in his judgement. As he drove along the loch-side road to the west coast harbour town, he found the scenery so breath-taking, and again had the sense of encroaching on someone else's kingdom.

When he reached the ferry terminal, he was more ener-gised than tired and sat on the bonnet of his car, studying the front of the town. It looked like others much closer to home, yet it felt different. The accents that drifted towards him gave it an exotic edge and made him wonder which of these, her kinsfolk, might be her friends, acquaintances, or even lovers.

He would like to be her lover tonight, although he did not imagine it would happen against the backdrop of what he'd come to tell her.

Watching the water churn as the boat on which he stood ploughed through it, James shuddered at the thought of meeting his end in the kind of waves that Walden conjured to seal his Shelagh's fate. For safety, he moved back from the railings and sat on a plastic chair bolted to the very middle of the deck.

He was glad to drive off the ferry and onto Mull where, even under the settling of cloud cover, the rise and fall of the land that was just beginning to succumb to the lure of autumn colours was a match for any great landscape. It seemed fitting to him that Ruth should come from a place of such beauty and mystery. Fitting yet disquieting because, if she had all of this, it seemed unlikely she would have much use for a divorced bookseller from Scarborough.

The feeling grew as he parked his car and walked aboard the smaller ferry that would take him across the slip of water separating Mull from Iona. Even from a distance he knew the latter was no ordinary place. The cloud that surrounded him with heavy, damp air, parted above the tiny island to create a crack of light that looked every bit like a stairway to heaven. This, he felt he knew, whether because he had read it or because he now saw it for himself, was not a place where angels feared to tread. He, however, knowing the bag on his shoulder contained news ugly enough to disturb the peace of this place, felt anything but angelic.

The fact that Ruth did not meet him off the ferry did nothing to assuage his insecurity. He hadn't really expected her to be there since he had lost his phone signal and therefore not called as agreed, but as he stepped off the boat into the unknown, he'd have been happy to be surprised.

He stood at the pier, taking in the low-lying houses sitting assuredly in their craggy green surrounds, before consulting the piece of paper on which he had scribbled Ruth's address before leaving home so many hours ago.

James had been expecting a longer walk and would have overshot his destination had it not been for a woman with shoulder-length fading red hair just opening her front door. She looked at him with the same curiosity he felt for the entire island, and spoke to him with a soft Scottish lilt.

"Hello. Can I help you?"

"Maybe. I'm looking for a bed and breakfast."

"We've a couple. Which one?"

"Sea View."

"You're here. Do you have a reservation?"

"No. I'm not staying here. I'm looking for Ruth... Ruth Morton."

"You've come to the right place. I'm Ruth's mother, Morna Morton."

He accepted the hand she extended, noting the firmness of her grasp.

"James Hunter, pleased to meet you."

As she gave him the once over, he hoped he didn't look as unclean as his long drive had left him feeling.

"If I'd known when you were coming, I'd have sent Ruth down to the pier to meet you."

"It's all right, I said I'd call but then my phone didn't work, so I... I'm here now."

"So you are. You'd better come on in."

"Thank you, Mrs Morton."

She led the way inside.

"You can call me Morna."

"And you can call me Jim."

"Right you are."

She showed him through the narrow hallway and into a cosy little kitchen where a fire was burning, its fumes mingling with the comforting lure of home cooking. He scanned his new surroundings, taking in four old chairs around a table in the centre of the room, a Welsh dresser with rows of blue-rimmed crockery, pans bubbling on a stove, a rocking chair, and a stack of newspapers and books piled on the floor beside it. On one wall there were three low windows set deep in stone mullions; on another there were paintings and photographs, one of which he could tell from a distance was of the woman who made his heart skip a beat.

"Put your bags over there, James... Jim, and then come and sit down. I'll see if I can find Ruth for you."

She disappeared, leaving him alone to admire the view. Until that moment, he had always thought the one from his office window special enough, particularly if he happened to be looking through it when the sun was either coming or going, but it had nothing on the sight he now beheld. He could see right across the water to Mull, which though fresh in his memory, was a world away from this house in which he now found himself. How much of Ruth it must have seen and how insignificant he felt within it.

"Hello."

He recognised the voice even before his memory could tell him who it belonged to, and spun around to meet it.

"Hello."

He walked towards her, unsure of the etiquette of such occasions. He wanted to hug her but didn't dare make the first move.

"You made it."

"Yes."

"Do you want to sit down?"

"Okay."

They sat at the kitchen table.

"How was your journey?"

"Fine. Thank you. It's probably not all that many miles, but it feels as if I've travelled half way around the world."

"Blame it on the sea. It has that effect on everyone."

"I'm not complaining though. It's spectacular."

"The island?"

"The island, this house, the sea, everything."

"I can show you around if you like."

"Around the house?"

"Or the island."

"Either would be good. Or both."

James considered taking the manuscript along with him, and finding a quiet spot to sit with her while she read it, or if she preferred, while he read it to her. But there was time yet. A little. He hoped.

- 61 -

He is livid. His journey, *travel for a day in France with Napoleonic marshal (7),* has not been smooth. The bad luck that prevented his early departure has escorted him all the way to Oban, the godforsaken town in which he now finds himself. His car has not performed as it should, and neither has the weather, which has been as brutally unkind to him as he would like to be to it.

He has accepted, during the course of the day, that he must adapt to the new circumstances, but he cannot accept what the woman behind the counter at the ferry ticket sales office is saying. She persists in telling him that she cannot sell him a ticket to get him anywhere before morning because the final ferry of the day has already left. He is insisting, in return, that he is not asking for a ride on the Titanic, *Giant in charge of sinking ship (7),* and that such a limited service is simply not good enough and certainly no good to him.

He tells her he has no time for silly women who sit at sales desks if they have nothing to sell, and even less for captains unwilling to bend the rules which on this occasion evidently need to be bent if he is to reach his destination. He tells her in no uncertain terms that he does not want her list of local accommodation because he will not, under any circumstances, be spending the night in the same town as her. He has other plans. He will be crossing, *Zebra angry with Dutch bank (8).*

He assures her that he will, if necessary, swim. He is a strong swimmer and afraid of neither distance nor darkness. She appears alarmed and at pains to stop him from going to such lengths to take to the waves, which she warns him are notoriously unpredictable. He counters that he is a match for an unruly basin of salt water, which is hardly an ocean, *No ace in this vast wet expanse (5)*, and that if she does not find a solution to his most pressing of problems, he will take her with him, although he is not quite so certain he would be able to swim all the way to Mull with human cargo, so might leave her to fend for herself en-route.

James looks taller than I remember, and nicer, too. He's wearing the same jumper he had on when we met, and I'm glad to see something I recognise. He doesn't hug me and I daren't make the first move, so to avoid standing staring at each other, I invite him to sit. But now we're sitting staring at each other and I'm wishing I'd suggested going for a walk instead. Apart from anything else, I have to tell him not to mention Walden in front of my mother before he hands me the manuscript while she is watching.

"I can show you around if you like."

"Around the house?"

I can hear Mum at the top of the stairs and therefore about to put an end to the three minutes of discretion she has granted us.

"Or the island."

"Either would be good. Or both."

She is half-way down now, and I'm on my feet, willing James not to say anything I would regret.

"Shall we go then?"

He stands and follows me into the hall.

"We're just going out for a walk, Mum."

She is on the bottom stair, her slippers looking worn in the face of company. I glance at James to see if he has no-ticed, but his eyes are nowhere near my mother's feet.

"You can't go out now, dinner's almost ready."

"We won't be long."

"Aye, but neither will dinner. Surely you can take a wee walk afterwards. And anyway, Jim must be tired out after all that travelling, I bet what he'd really like now is a nice cup of tea."

Jim? Who said she could call him Jim?

"That sounds lovely Morna, thank you."

And who said he could call her Morna?

"Come on then the pair of yous, into the kitchen."

She turns to James.

"You sit yourself down and Ruth will make the tea, won't you dear?"

She leaves me little choice.

"Of course. What kind would you like?"

"Whatever you've got."

My mother is looking at me as if I've taken leave of my senses.

"We've only got plain old tea here."

"My favourite kind."

James is sitting and he looks more comfortable than I feel.

"Where are you from, Jim?"

"Scarborough."

"In Lancashire?"

"Yorkshire."

"Of course it is. I went there once. Long time ago now, mind you. I seem to remember a big hotel on a cliff top. Didn't it fall into the sea? I'm sure I heard something like that."

I almost give myself away by jumping to the defence of the hotel to which James took me. It doesn't seem right that she should even be aware of the existence of the building in which he undressed me, and even less so that she should think it in the sea.

"You heard right. Part of a hotel fell into the sea about fifteen years ago." He looks at me.

"But there's another one on another cliff. It's called the Grand Hotel, and it used to be the biggest in Europe. I stayed there once. Found it very memorable."

If she looks at me now she'll be able to use the colour in my face and neck to answer several of her questions about me and James. I risk a glance in his direction, and find him staring right at me. He smiles, then turns to my mother.

"Can I do anything to help?"

"Absolutely not. You stay where you are."

"Thank you."

"Not at all. It'd be a poor do if I couldn't even offer you a wee cup of tea and a bite to eat after such a long journey."

"It's very kind."

"Like I said, dinner almost ready. Ruth, if you could set the table after you've made the tea please."

"Okay."

"And remember to set it for four."

She turns to James. "I have a paying guest tonight and I always offer a meal when they're arriving late. I've often thought I should call my place a B&B&D... Did you come all the way from Scarborough today?"

"I did."

"Just to see Ruth?"

"Yes."

He's looking at me, and I'm grateful to him for not mentioning Walden.

"That's nice. So come on then, Jim, tell me how you two know each other?"

She's out of control.

"Mu-um."

"What?"

"We should check him into the hotel before it gets too late. We've got time for that now, haven't we – seeing as how your guest isn't here yet."

"Nonsense, you can do it afterwards. Or are you in a particular hurry, Jim?"

I wish she'd stop calling him that.

"I... I can do it now or... whatever best suits."

"I think later would be better. Ruth can show you the way after we've eaten. Give you a chance to catch up on... well, on whatever you need to catch up on."

I steal a glance in his direction, expecting to see traces of annoyance at my mother's approach, but he's smiling as if he means it.

"That sounds great."

"Pour him a cup of tea then, Ruth."

There's an instructive tone to her voice that prevents me from doing anything other than what she says. I take him his cup, feeling like an outsider tending to my mother's oldest friend rather than to my own newest.

"Thanks. Are you sure I can't help at all?"

"I don't think so."

"We wouldn't hear of it, Jim. You just relax. Read the paper if you like. Ruth and I will take care of everything else."

She simultaneously drags me to the stove and our standing as women of equal rights into the dark ages. She hasn't let me near her pans all afternoon so I don't know what she wants me to do here now.

"Someone likes the crossword, I see."

"Och aye, I love them. I didn't get far with it today mind. I was too busy. Do you do them yourself?"

"Sometimes. I can just about manage the quick one, but I'm not exactly what you'd call a dab-hand at the cryptic."

"They're easy enough once you get the hang of the formula. I say if I can do it, anyone can."

"Okay, so what's the formula then? Tell me how did you turn *Some French have very small following but make a lot* into *Destiny.*"

I'm trying to remember when I last saw mum with one of my friends. It must have been a long time ago, and I'm fairly sure it wasn't like this. I should be glad she likes him, and somewhere inside, I'm sure I am. But I feel as though I'm crashing their party, whereas in actual fact, she's crashing mine. And more to the point, preventing me from asking James for the manuscript that brought him here.

"Oh, that was an easy one. I'll show you after dinner. Not that we'll be having any if you don't set the table Ruth."

"I'm just getting the plates out."

"Four, remember?"

"I remember. What time are you expecting your guest?"

"Any minute now, I'd imagine."

- 6 3 -

He has used the force of his charms to extract from the ferry ticket saleswoman the names and contact details of private boatmen who might offer him a passage. He has plenty of money so is in no doubt that he will succeed in hiring someone to do the job and get him to the bed he has booked to stay in. The weather is blacker than his mood, but his mood catches up with each phone call he places to the sailors on his list. They would be fools, they claim one by one, to venture back out to sea on such a windy night unless they absolutely had to. Only a coward, *Draw back after commanding officer finds one with fear (6),* he tells them in the same order, would turn down the sum of money he is offering for a short trip across mildly choppy water. But their trepidation, *Apprehension comes from shaking tepid ration (11),* is greater than them, and the only thing to be swayed are the boats they will not steer from their moorings.

By the time his anger has cut the line between him and the last scaredy cat, *Felix is frightened perhaps (7, 3),* he telephones, the sea is dancing savagely in response to the winds that thrash it.

He, however, is not deterred. He has no fear, *Echo in distance causes fright (4).* He meant what he said when he told the ticket saleswoman that he would not be hanging his hat in the same town as her. He retrieves the fishing rods from his car and, still wearing the suit he put on first thing this morning, strides to the beach from where he can see a number of smaller vessels swaying in the shallow water. His mood lifts slightly as he approaches the boat of his choice, a lightweight vessel with oars he won't need and an outboard motor he certainly will. He checks under the seat for a fuel canister, and feels his mood lift again when he realises that by the same time tomorrow, the very sea in which he now floats will have claimed the life he has come to end.

- 6 4 -

Morna Morton was immediately taken with James. Any preconceived notion of him she had time to form was shattered by the brown-haired Yorkshire man sitting in her kitchen talking about crossword puzzles. Although she thought his overall appearance would be improved were he to comb his hair and treat himself to a new jumper, she believed he possessed exactly the kind of ease and warmth she had never been able to give Ruth, and which she firmly believed would stand him in good stead as a fine father.

She very much hoped that role would go to James rather than Mr Walden and, from her place at the cooker, kept one eye on him, hoping to see him stroke Ruth's belly. He did not do that, but there was no doubt in Morna's eyes that his were filled with affection for her daughter, and that he was a man willing to go a long way - a lot further than Iona - to be with her.

What she was less sure about, however, was Ruth's feelings for him. The speed with which she had tried to get him out of the house and checked into his hotel, without so much as a cup of tea, had not been lost on her. Likely as not, Ruth would have had the poor man eating alone in the village had Morna not been there to insist he dine with them.

She found him a willing partner in conversation, and had they been alone, she could well have imagined that, by the end of dinner, she'd have had known a lot more than she currently did. But as it was, Ruth was hovering around, neither entertaining him nor helping her, and evidently needed some guidance of her own.

"Are you going to set the table Ruth dear?"

"I'm just getting the plates out."

"Four, remember?"

"I remember. What time are you expecting your guest?"

"Any minute now, I'd imagine."

Actually, she'd expected a knock at the door a good half hour earlier and a small part of her was hoping Tod Walden might not show up at all, for his arrival would certainly alter the intimacy of the current trio. Then again, she needed to see him to know she was right to back her instinct's bet, so decided to use what time she had with Jim to find out whatever she could that might help keep the odds in his favour.

"So Jim, what do you do?"

"I run a mail order book business."

"How interesting. Do you enjoy your work?"

"I do."

"And do you manage to make a good living from it?"

"Keeps me busy."

"And it's work you can do from anywhere, I presume."

"I don't know. I've only ever tried it from Scarborough."

"A change is as good as a rest."

- 65 -

My mother is unstoppable. James has only been here for five minutes and she's practically asking him for bank statements and telling him to relocate. I look at him and hope he can see my apology somewhere in and amongst my embarrassment. I need to get him out of the room before she pushes him out of my life.

"Would you like a tour of the house?"

"Excellent idea."

"We'll be back in a minute, mum."

"Okay. Don't go messing up the guest room though, he should be here any second."

We go out of the kitchen and cross the tiny hallway into the living room.

"Your mum's great." I look at him to see if he's joking, but he doesn't seem to be. "So friendly."

"She can be."

"I guess it must be true what they say about the Scots."

"What? That we're stingy and ask people we've just met how much they earn?"

"That you're very welcoming."

He's looking right at me and is close enough for me to pick up his soapy smell. It carries me away to Scarborough and being in his arms in the pub. I look at them hanging by his sides, his hands hidden under the sleeves that are too long, and I wish he would wrap them around me. "It's good to see you again Ruth."

I must be blushing. I put my hand up to my neck.

"It's nice to see you too."

"You look lovely."

"I… it's a really old dress."

"Still lovely."

I am in Scarborough again. It sends a shiver through me to think that I have been naked with this man.

"Thank you."

"I should have brought you flowers or something. But it was a bit of a spontaneous decision. Bit unlike me, that."

He seems shy standing here, and the room I know so well is unfamiliar with him in it. As if his presence has rearranged everything.

"I… I wanted to ask you if you–'

"If I brought the photocopies? I did."

"Thank you. But I wanted to ask if you could not mention Walden in front of my mother."

"I didn't, did I?"

"No you didn't. And I don't want you to."

"Okay. No problem. I won't mention him. Walden's the word. Does that mean you haven't told her about the book?"

"No I haven't. I don't know what's going on with her, she seems confused about things."

"About Walden?"

"About all sorts of things, including him. I told you she keeps mentioning his name, but she also says she knows nothing about him. And I don't think she's lying."

He takes a step towards me, and takes my hands in his.

"Ruth, you have to read the rest of the book. There are things in it that might help you make sense of everything, things that might help you understand your mother's–"

"Are you two nearly finished?"

She appears in the doorway.

"Oh, I'm sorry, I don't mean to disturb, but I think we should eat. Jim, would you mind carving? It'd be nice to have a man do the honours for once."

"I'd be happy to oblige."

He looks at me and mouths the words "I'll tell you later." He lets go of my hands, turns, and leaves. I take my time walking the few metres to the kitchen, and sit down just as my mother is putting the roast chicken on the table. She hands James the carving knife.

"I'll bet the moment we lift our knives and forks, there'll be a knock on the door… Ruth, there's no salt on the table, could you fetch it over?"

James starts to carve into the meat. I see his hands at work, but I don't allow my eyes to wander up to his face.

"Ruth? Did you hear what I said? We'll be needing the salt. Oh never mind, I'll get it myself."

James carves deftly. He's done this before, and a few moments ago I might have enjoyed watching him, but now my thoughts are on the words he left me with, and the manuscript which must be in his bag by the fire.

"It's a juicy looking bird, isn't it Jim?"

"It is indeed. Just as well. You could do with a bit of fattening up, and I'm sure Ruth must be hungry. She's barely eaten a thing all day."

"I'm not really."

"Nonsense, you've got to keep your strength up."

"Your mum's right, Ruth."

I chance a look at him. He winks at me as he smiles, and the gesture reaches right inside me, chasing out some of the fear. I push my plate towards him.

"Just a little bit."

"What about you Morna?"

"One of the drumsticks and wee bit of the breast would be grand. And it looks like it'll just be the three of us after all. The last ferry must be long gone by now, and it doesn't take more than three minutes to get here from the pier."

"Maybe he got lost. I almost walked straight past."

"He'd have had to get very lost at that rate."

The last word leaves her lips in unison with the sound of the doorbell.

"What did I say? Didn't I say this would happen? Will you get it, Ruth?"

I'm not in the mood to make small talk with a stranger, and wish that whoever he is, he hadn't made it here, and wouldn't be about to enter my mother's kitchen and spend the night in my bed. I wish that all the more when he demonstrates his impatience by ringing the bell for the second time.

"Hello Ruth dear, I heard you were back."

"Hello Betty."

"Oh, it's you."

My mother has appeared behind me.

"Aye, it's only me. Although I normally get a nicer welcome than that."

Betty has managed to wriggle her way inside without being invited.

"Don't take it to heart, I was just expecting someone else, that's all."

"So I see. It's not often you've got your table set for four, Morna."

"No. Well this is Jim, he's a friend of Ruth's. Jim, this is Betty, Betty Jenner. And we're expecting a paying guest tonight as well. I thought he'd be coming in off the last boat."

"That came in about twenty minutes ago."

"Aye, that's what I was just saying. Ruth thinks he might have got lost."

"I doubt that. D'you mind if I sit a moment, Morna? Yous carry on eating, don't let me get in the way. I've just been having a bit of trouble with my knee, and it'd be good to rest for a wee moment before I set off back home. Aye, that's better. So, Ruthy, is this your boyfriend then? He's very handsome."

- 66 -

James Hunter had always been a great believer in first impressions, and Morna made a good one. He liked her aura of calm chaos and the way she asked him frank questions as if their meeting were any but the first. She had a generosity of spirit, he could see that, which made it all the harder for him to imagine her deserving of the fate Walden had sketched out for her in the concluding pages of his book.

Sitting in the little kitchen with Ruth and her mother, watching them with each other, he felt a profound sense of responsibility. He, he firmly believed, was the only one who knew of Walden's plans except for the plotter himself, and it was therefore up to him to break the news, and to break it as gently as he could. The last thing he wanted was to be cast out of Morna's home or Ruth's affections. Not least because from the outside, he feared there would be less he could do to protect either one or the other of them.

Choosing his moment was not easy. He knew he could not simply bluster into their home and hand them information that would render its walls rubble around them. He needed a little time with them first, time that was easily filled with the comforting sounds and smells of cooking, time that moved faster than him.

His thought his opening had come when Ruth took him into the living room and told him she was worried about her mother's references to Walden. But it closed again before he could get through it, and left him in the awkward position of having dropped a hint which lingered between him and Ruth for the duration of the chicken dinner he had been asked to carve. He was therefore relieved to hear the doorbell herald the opportunity for distraction all round.

Betty, it turned out, didn't so much offer him distraction as drive him to it. When she had first appeared and insisted that the B&B guest for whom a place had been dutifully laid was evidently not coming after all, he hoped he might be invited to use the empty room. But when he involuntarily began to rub his ears more than usual, he recognised it as a symptom of his need to escape Betty's love of her own voice. As such, Ruth's offer to show him to his hotel came as sweet relief, and grabbing his bag containing the photocopies of *The Ruthlessness of One Man*, they headed out into the blanket of night.

"But you promise to come back and have breakfast with us in the morning, Jim. There's no need to eat in a restaurant full of strangers when you have friends along the road."

"You try and stop me."

"Good. Will you be long Ruth?"

"I don't think so."

He was touched by the way Ruth addressed her answer as much to him as to her mother, and more as a question than a statement of fact.

"It might be nice to get a breath of sea air. If you can spare her that long?"

"Aye, that's not a problem. I've got Betty to keep me company."

James and Ruth walked in silence for a few moments, the former unable to decide whether to break it with a comment about Walden or a moonlight kiss. Half way to the hotel, Ruth took the decision from him.

"You were saying something about my mother and Walden's book."

"I was."

"What?"

"Do you want me to tell you or do you want to read it for yourself?"

"Both. Tell me what I need to know, and then I'll read it."

"Okay. But can I ask you something first? I know I keep saying that…"

"Sure. Go on."

"Where's your father?"

- 6 7 -

He has not been at the helm of a boat for many years and is out of practice, and maybe out of his depth. The waves are higher than is suitable for the vessel he has borrowed, and the outboard light is too dim to burn very far through the darkness. He congratulates himself on having brought a map of the islands with him, and knows that if he follows the shoreline he will be spared the worst of the weather and be certain to reach Iona and the woman who calls herself Morna and who owes him a life.

He is appalled that she should have chosen a place of religious sanctity to hide from him and will tell her before her lungs fill with salty water that living among Christians will not make her one, and that her home is in the furnaces of hell.

During the choppy crossing he entertains himself with thoughts of what she will look like now as compared to then, when she was supported by youth, *So, few years are in you then? (5)*. He laughs at the prospect of the havoc certain to have been reaped upon her by the process of age-ing, *Spirit is shaken at end of epoch - or just time passing by (5)*. He wipes the spray from his suit, which is now sod-den, and smoothes back his hair; hair he is sure she would no longer have were she a man.

He knows time will not have been as kind to her, be-cause she does not deserve kindness from anyone or anything. He imagines her as a surly, burly old woman who can no longer walk without sticks. He does not relish the prospect of pretending to be there to proclaim his love for her all over again, but that is part of the plan and cannot therefore be changed.

He remembers with waves of bitterness as great as those of salt water lashing his boat, the promises she made him. He remembers, too, all the trips he made in search of her after they had been broken. And he curses her, the girl now an old woman, who came from nowhere and vanished into thin air. Three decades on, that air has assumed a form. It is a patch of land, less than foursquare miles, surrounded by the beauty of difficult escape. And when the night sky that squats around him finally rises to yield day, he will step onto that land and take what is his.

- 6 8 -

Morna Morton was pensive as she boiled the bones of the chicken that Betty Jenner had continued to eat long after the others had put down their forks. She was very fond of her friend, but that did not make her immune to the woman's less endearing habits, the most noticeable of which was regularly outstaying her welcome.

Tonight, however, she was too busy wondering why Tod Walden had not turned up, and whether Jim's arrival on the island had anything to do with his sudden change of heart. Not that she minded. She had been impressed by Jim and had enjoyed watching him carve her fowl, so much so that she had allowed herself the liberty of imagining him assuming the same responsibility on a regular basis. She was just trying to picture the faceless Mr Walden doing the same when her daughter opened the front door.

"Hello dear, I was starting to wonder where you were."

Ruth entered the living room and sat down, looking wretched enough for Morna to assume she must have had an altercation with Jim.

"Are you all right?"

"Mother, I need to talk to you about something."

"Do you? What is it?"

"Where's my father?"

- 69 -

I'm home. I need to see my mother, to find out if any of what James has read to me is based on a truth kept out of my reach. There is no easy introduction to the subject, there is only the question itself. I ask it, then have to clench my teeth to try and steady the tremble of my head, as I wait for her response.

"Your father?"

All I can manage is a nod.

"He's dead. You know that."

"Are you sure?"

"What do you mean? He drowned after you were born. You know he did."

A familiar tone of discomfort has crept into her voice, a tone I always understood to be born of her sadness. But tonight, I wonder if it has another origin. She looks small and fragile perched on the edge on the sofa opposite me.

"Because if he isn't dead…"

"He is."

"It's been a long day, and I'm tired. If you don't mind I think I'm going to go to bed."

"Mum?"

"What is it?"

"Don't go… please. I really need to talk with you."

"I've said all there is to say on the subject."

"It's something else. Will you sit down for a moment?"

She takes a moment to turn back and join me, but when she does, her eyes are wild with anticipation, and she's smiling. She sits on the sofa, comfortably this time. My head is shaking again, as if its weight were too much for my neck to bear.

"What is it?"

"It's about James."

"Yes?"

"And Mr Walden."

"Yes?"

The tremors have spread to other parts of my body, and she must be able to tell.

"Don't fret, dear. You can tell me, I'm your mother."

"Okay. Well Mr Walden is a writer. You already know that, although for the life of me I still don't understand how you read an article about him. But what I want to tell, have to tell you, is that he wrote a book for me."

"That's nice."

"No. No, it is not nice. It is not a nice book… There are things in the book… things about me and about… about you."

"About me?"

"Yes."

The confusion on her face betrays her age, and I look away.

"What do you mean? What kind of things?"

"I don't want you to be upset by this, but he thinks he's my father and that you hid me from him."

I'm looking at her again, but she doesn't allow my eyes to rest on hers. This time she turns away, her mouth slightly parted as if about to speak. But she doesn't. Not for several long and empty moments, moments I fill with the possibility of having a father.

"I see."

"You see? What do you see? Is it true? Is Mr Walden my father?"

She turns to look at me square on.

"No."

"Mum, you can tell me if he is. If there's something you want to tell me… anything… I won't be upset."

She's staring at me, her eyes like glass, giving nothing away.

"Your father is dead, Ruth. He died a very long time ago. So whatever this Mr Walden has been saying, it is not true. Do you understand me?"

"Yes."

"He's dead. He died after you were born. And his name family name was Law. I don't understand why... why are you asking me all this?"

"I just wondered. I suppose I've always wondered why we don't have any photographs of him, and why I never met his parents?"

"You know why. We don't have any pictures because I never did. And you had no grandparents because Ned was estranged from them, and because they were not nice people. Is that a good enough answer for you? Or would you prefer to believe what a stranger writes in a book? Because if you do..."

"No, I... I'm sorry for bringing it up. We don't have to talk about it anymore."

"Good."

Now she's the one trembling. I can't remember the last time I saw my mother cry, or if I ever have. I drag myself to the sofa to provide as much physical comfort as is possible between us.

"I didn't want to upset you. Really. I think having a stalker is clouding my judgement."

She looks up at me with bloodshot eyes, tears pouring down her face.

We don't hug very much, and my arm feels awkward around her, but she doesn't resist. She reaches her hand up to mine and holds it tight. As we sit, I decide not to tell her that Walden is planning to come to the island, and certainly not what he wants to do when he gets here. I don't think she's strong enough for that.

Morna Morton's mind was working hard to understand all the ramifications of what her daughter was telling her. There was a Mr Walden, a writer, who, far from being romantically involved with Ruth, believed he was her father. This not only meant that the investigator had given her incorrect information, and that there was likely no baby, but that Ruth's reason for coming to Iona was to run away from the man she called her stalker. Morna suspected that might count as a silver lining, but could not yet see clearly enough to know for sure.

What she could see, however, was that both she and Ruth were in grave danger. The memories of her escape came rushing back to her like a burst dam. She had not cried like that since the months leading up to the birth of the baby-turned-woman now holding her hand. And as they sat together, she thought hard about her next move.

She could not possibly tell Ruth the truth about Walden without losing both her dignity and her daughter. Neither was she willing to let on that the man who had all but kept her under lock and key for her last year in London had been planning – and God alone knew how he had tracked them down – to spend the night in her house. But she had to do something, so she sat still, clutching Ruth's hand while she thought hard about her next move.

"Does Jim know about the book?"

"Yes. It's a long story, but he's been trying to help me find out who Walden is."

"I see."

Morna didn't need to know any more than that in order to decide what to do next. She would go to Jim and implore him to get Ruth off the island. She would not tell him her whole sorry story; she had sworn she would never tell anyone that. But she would let him know that the guest who missed the ferry went by the name of Mr Walden and that given his evident insanity, it could only be sensible to get out of his way. If Jim thought it wise to share that information with Ruth, then so be it. She would tell him she had opted not to on the grounds that Ruth had enough to worry about already.

She would go very early. She knew the hotel staff and would not have any difficulty finding out his room number. If she got there by 6 a.m. that would still give the two of them a couple of hours to get organised before the first ferry over to Mull. From there, they could take Jim's car and go far away. She would give them the money she had under her mattress, and she would stay at home and wait for the man of her nightmares to reappear.

She would wait up to her neck and beyond in fear but she would do so remembering the vow she had made to herself to prevent Ned Law from ever laying another finger on the child he so violently co-created.

- 7 1 -

He has run out of fuel and he wishes he were a god. As such, he would power his pathetic craft across the sea with the force of his fury. But he is not a god, and his fury is tying him up in knots rather than propelling him across the water at a rate thereof.

He has also run out of options. He will have to row the rest of the way which, although by his estimations cannot be more than another five miles, given his unwelcome yet undeniable fatigue, will take him longer than it will for the sun to rise. Until day breaks, he will also have to venture further away from the rocky shoreline, as travelling with his back to his destination in the dark would prevent him from seeing anything that might sink him and his mission before he is able to draw it to its natural conclusion.

He wends his way out into the wider waters and wilder winds, challenging his muscles to keep him moving. As they do, he occupies his mind with crossword clues that literally live up to their name. Fury, *Mythical singleton sees red (4)*. Wrath, *Cross ghostly figure with no eye to make Scottish outerwear? (5)*. Rage, *Sun god needs power company added to show off his anger (4)*. Grump, *One's mood deteriorates in frying rump steak (5)*. Indignant, *Is Di tanning - or just affronted (9)*.

- 72 -

It is 5.05 a.m. My mother is in her bed, and I am in mine, in sheets washed and ironed for a guest who failed to show. I know my mother is asleep because I can hear the gentle rhythm of her snores through the wall. It makes me wonder if I snore like that. Tonight I wish I did, because that would signify sleep, which I want. But sleep does not want me. I pass the drag of time with thoughts of James, who is just a few hundred metres from where I lie. I imagine him in the bed on which we sat side by side earlier this evening. There was no repeat of what happened in Scarborough, but there was a single kiss, caution, kindness and care.

I shall be glad to see him again in the morning. I will go to him before he has the chance to do as my mother insisted and join us for breakfast. I will take him up on his offer of helping to convince her to join me in leaving the island while he lays in wait for the man who planned her fatal accident, and who I have just learned has something else in store for me.

A full and respectful week passed between Shelagh's death and burial, and after Davina and Tod had closed the door on the last of the mourners to leave the wake, they sat down together to the celebratory dinner she insisted on making for them. The mood danced with the promise of the unknown, of the unknown promise he would soon make to her. In the unimaginative eyes of the law he could not be her betrothed, but what the law could not see, it could not imagine.

He did not get down on one knee to make the proposal to which her only answer could be "yes", but held her hands across the table and pledged, Dear Reader, to take the very best care of her from that day forth and until death drove them apart. It came as no surprise to him to see her beautiful green eyes, eyes that he had helped to make, fill with the same joy he felt at the prospect of their future.

Davina, anxious to embark upon it as quickly as possible, and even before dessert had been served, questioned Tod about where they would live. He assured her he had a wonderful home waiting for her. He would be taking her a safe distance from the white sands of her deprived childhood, far from the island off whose shores her mother met with the fate she so deserved, to a home where they would be alone, where she would want for nothing and no-one, because she would have him. And with him, she would do what all good books promise. She would live happily ever after.

- 73 -

He has arrived, and in better time than he thought. The winds of the night have dropped to a whisper and he is pleased to see that day has broken over perfect fishing conditions. He knew from his topographical research of Iona that it has several beaches and though it cost him extra effort and energy to get there, he opted to come aground at the back of the island, facing out into the vastness of the Atlantic.

He rows to the shore, *Alternative within her beside the seaside (5)*. His arms and legs twitching with the exertion of the journey, he drags his boat onto the sand, *Gritty new conjunctions! (4)*, where it will stay until he comes back later to claim it for an afternoon spent bobbing about in the coastal waters of the North Atlantic.

He trusts his sense of direction to take him to her mother's house, as profoundly as he trusts his charm to secure him the old bag's affections once he gets there. He anticipates his arrival in the two women's lives, savouring the reactions he imagines will be theirs: the mother's for the surprise it will contain, and hers for the gratitude. For a second he wonders whether she will have told her mother about his book, but only for a second, because he trusts her to keep their secret, even if she did not do as he said and travel to Scotland with him.

He walks over rocks, *Odd bottle stoppers seem stony! (5)*, and along the pathway towards the house, his suit, damp from the salt spray, clinging to him. He passes sheep at which he bleats mockingly. When they respond with a sound to echo his own, he runs at them, stamping his feet.

He takes a particular dislike to a black-faced one and to demonstrate his contempt, picks up a large stone and throws it at the animal. He is pleased to see that his aim is as good as ever and walks on leaving the sheep to lick its wound.

He is expecting the old bag to open the door to the house, which is every bit as twee as he imagined, and is rehearsing his opening and vomitive line about how life was never quite the same without her, when he suddenly finds himself staring into the same pretty face he has been studying through his telescope for so many months.

He is struck by her in-the-flesh good looks and visible excitement at his arrival. He does not need to introduce himself, because he knows she knows who he is, but he cannot resist.

"Hello Davina. How nice to meet you after all these years."

He passes by her silence and walks into the living room, which he is sickened to find decorated in pale pink, and home to a floral sofa, *Where muddled oafs may sit (4)*. He lowers himself onto the insipid object, beckoning her to follow his lead, and is happy that she so willingly obliges.

"Don't you have anything to say to me?"

"I... Mr Walden?"

"You may call me father."

"Hello."

He leans towards her to get a closer look at the fabric of her face, and lifts his left hand to the deep red hair he would have liked to brush for her as a small girl.

"I would prefer 'hello father.'"

He strokes her hair with a softness he never received from his own parents, and savours the experience for as long as it takes for him to remember he is in the old bag's house and that she must be in it too.

"Did you like my book?"

"I..."

"Yes father... I knew you would. I trust your mother knows nothing about it."

"No."

"No? Does that means you told her or not?"

"No... no, I didn't."

He points at a picture of two elderly looking ladies on the mantelpiece. "She never was much of a looker. Hard to imagine I ever got carnal with her. Where is she?"

"She's still sleeping."

He cannot see why, as she is too ugly to find sleep remotely beneficial. Her absence, conversely, is, as it affords him the chance to talk to Davina about the rowing excursion scheduled for later that day.

- 74 -

Walden is here. I am sitting a few feet from him in my mother's living room, while she is asleep upstairs. Had he knocked just a minute later, I would have been on my way to the hotel to talk to James, and she would have been alone in her home with this strange man who insists I call him "father", and whose fingers are now touching my hair.

I am doing everything I can to smother the scream rising from deep within me. I want to let it out and run far, far away from its cause, whose foul breath and icy eyes are all over my face.

In my mind, Walden was nothing like the dishevelled grey-haired man at my side. He was creepy, but he was small and neat and had a tidy moustache. The real him is redder of face. He is telling me he forgives me for coming to the island by myself, but that from now on, we must work together, no matter how many people try to intervene to prevent what has to be.

I feel the nod of my head, which is rendered weightless by the blood and comprehension that have left it. All I can think is that I have to find a way to get him out of here before my mother wakes up. He is clearly out of his mind, and who knows what he will do when she refuses, as I am certain she will, to go fishing with him. I have to get him to James, who I hope will know what to do.

"We have so much to talk about, Davina. Did your mother ever tell you that is your real name? It means loved one. Did she ever tell you about me?"

He is looking right at me through eyes that don't understand human kindness. His frown is scored deep into his
forehead, and his cheeks are hollow with anger.

"I would like to embrace you."

He is moving even closer to me bringing his smell and
the hardness of his expectations with him. I do not want to
be hugged by this man, not for a second.

"We could go for a walk."

"Did you not hear me? I said I would like to embrace
you."

He is standing and is indicating to me that I should do
the same.

I stand up and let him put his arms around me. His grip
is tighter than is natural and my instincts are yelling at me
to break free of him. But my head tells me to stay where I
am, to give him what he wants for as long as it takes to get
him to James. So we stand there in my mother's living
room, his arms around me, mine limp at my sides. I can see
us in the reflection in the window – his arms rigid around
me, me limp in them. His eyes are closed. He is pushing his
head against me, rubbing his hair on mine. I don't want to
cry and I don't want to be sick, but the longer he holds me,
the greater the possibility of both become.

"I will never let you go again." He kisses my head.
"There, there. Everything's okay. I'm here now."

He pulls me tighter.

"I have been waiting for this moment for a very long
time."

I nod, because that, I sense, is what he wants me to do.

"Your mother will be surprised to see me."

I try to loosen his grip on me.

"Did she ever tell you anything about me?"

"I… she…"

"Did she tell you I was dead?"

"I… I was led to believe–"

"That I drowned? That's what she told me she'd say?"

His voice is low with spite. He has pulled away now,
and is looking at me with chilling anger. He is walking to
the sideboard, on which there are other photographs, this
time of me as a child.

"Can I get you a cup of tea?"

He is lifting the photos one at a time, scrutinising them, his lip curling with danger.

"Mr Walden?"

He turns to me.

"Tod Walden is only my pen name. My real name is Edward Law. Some call me Ned, but you, as I already said, must call me father."

I say nothing. I will call him nothing. He is not my father. I do not have a father. I never have had and I never will.

"Would you like a cup of tea?"

"No. I don't care for tea. I chose the name Tod for your mother. It means dead. *Sie ist Tod.* She is dead."

He sits back down, humming distractedly to himself as he picks up the newspaper from the coffee table.

"And she got this clue wrong. *To seek fortune, start bottom right and finish in a bible lesson with deep sympathy,* eleven letters. The answer should be *serendipity.*

"I thought I had that one wrong."

Walden and I both spin round to see my mother standing in the doorway. She is wearing her coat and boots and a smile the breadth of our island. For the split second it takes for my conscious mind to compute the implications, I am relieved to see her.

"Mum? I thought you were in bed."

"Not at all. I've been up for hours. Who's your guest? It's awful early for a visitor."

Walden stands and walks towards her, his dubious hand outstretched and reaching for her own. I move so I'm closer to her than he is.

"This is–"

"Come now Shelagh, don't be coy. You remember me."

Shelagh? My mother is looking at him blankly. As am I.

"Mum, this is Mr Walden."

I turn my head so that only she can see my face, which is urging her, begging her not to let on that she knows anything about who he is. Her own expression does not change. It acknowledges nothing.

"Good morning Mr Walden. I'm Morna Morton."

I can see her hand shaking as she extends it towards him, and my impulse is to steady her arm for her, to put mine back around her as I did last night.

"No need to pretend with me, Shelagh."

"I'm sorry, but have we met?"

"Have we met?"

His voice is slow and low and moves us onto a more openly threatening plane.

"You are my wife and you stole my baby."

75

Morna Morton heard Mr Walden before she saw him. Not
wanting to wake Ruth on her return from her dawn excursion to petition Jim, she had opened the door as quietly as
she knew how, and had been about to cross the threshold
when she heard her daughter's and a man's voice. She could
see nothing from where she stood, but she didn't need to in
order to know he had finally found her, and that no good
could come of it.

She cursed herself now for not going back to Jim to tell
him to come to the house immediately rather than in the
half hour they had agreed upon, but all she had been able to
think once she knew that Ruth was alone with the man who
so systematically abused her, was that she must go inside
and continue to protect the only good thing to come from
their tortured time together all those years ago. So in she
had gone.

Give nothing away, were the three words she had re-
peated as she walked into the living room armed with her
best smiles for both father and daughter.

"Good morning Mr Walden. I'm Morna Morton."

"No need to pretend with me, Shelagh."

"I'm sorry, but have we met?"

"Have we met? ... You stole my baby."

"I'm sorry, but you clearly have me confused with
someone else."

Morna knew she was playing a dangerous game with a
dangerous man, but she had to play it for as long as it took
Jim to get to the house and hopefully have the sense to go
and get help.

"Don't trifle with me Shelagh. I have had a long journey, and I've come to tell you all is forgiven and that I am willing to try again."

"That's very kind of you Mr Walden, and I'm sure the lady your offer is intended for will be delighted. But you must believe me when I tell you, it is not me."

"Now you listen to me, Shelagh. You might be fooling Davina, but you are not fooling me."

"Who on earth is Davina?" Morna looked at Ruth searchingly, "Ruth, go and put the kettle on would you? I think our guest could use a cup of tea."

"But…"

"Please just do as I ask."

Morna's tone was firm and left no space for Ruth to argue.

"We don't want Mr Walden to feel unwelcome now, do we?"

Once her daughter left the room, Morna gave the guest her full, if hushed, attention.

"I'm afraid your booking was for last night, Mr Walden. We have no vacancies tonight."

"You can stop the pretence now Shelagh. She knows everything, and she's willing to forgive you. So am I. Which is why I'm here. I want to be your partner again. Just you and me and Davina."

"Who is Davina?"

"Do not play games with me, Shelagh. You know very well who she is. My beloved Davina. You are lucky I never stopped looking for you. Lucky I spotted her. Lucky she led me back to you. And here I am, willing to forgive you no matter how unforgivable your leaving me."

"Why don't we just get you a nice cup of tea and I can phone around some of the other guest houses on the island to see if they have any vacancies…"

"That's enough Shelagh, I have travelled a hell of a long way to offer you a second chance, and I am not going to take no for an answer. And to mark our new beginning I shall be taking you out on a romantic fishing trip."

Morna recognised in his face the same venom that had periodically visited her in nightmares over the past thirty years, and she had serious doubts about the efficiency of her strategy. But there was no way to back out of it now.

"That's very kind of you Mr Walden, although it would hardly be appropriate for us to go on a romantic fishing trip when we have only just met. Now if you'll excuse me for a moment... I'll just see how the tea is coming on."

76

I've been straining to hear the conversation over the sound of the kettle my mother sent me to boil, and I've heard enough to know I have to get her out of Walden's reach. I turn back to the teapot when she announces she's coming to see how I'm getting on. She walks into the room, looking terrified. She glances behind her and then takes me by the arm and drags us both towards the window out of Walden's line of vision.

"Go and get Jim."

"I'm not leaving you here on your own."

"Ruth, I am not arguing with you…" The urgency in her voice is disturbing, and does nothing to help keep me calm.

"Who is Jim?"

We both turn around to where Walden is standing, breathing impatience into the kitchen through pursed lips. My mother beats me to a response.

"And, how do you take your tea?"

"I don't want tea. I want to prepare for our fishing trip, and I want Davina to help me."

He offers me a terse smile. I look from him to my mother, who is shaking her head almost imperceptibly. I know what I have to do.

"I'll get my shoes on."

"I'm coming with you."

My mother has linked her arm through mine in a way foreign to us both, and it feels uncomfortably comforting.

"No you aren't."

As he speaks, my mother's grip tightens on my arm.

"Your preparations will be wasted, because I will not be joining you to fish."

I have always known my mother to be determined, but have never thought her foolishly so. Not until this moment. Every word she speaks is winding Walden up more tightly, and that can't be clever. I need to get her out of the way and she needs to get James.

"It's all right, mum. You stay here. We won't be long."

I squeeze her arm with my own.

"And aren't you having breakfast at the hotel?"

I slowly pull my arm out of hers. She is reluctant to let go.

"Davina, I'm waiting."

"Where will you be?" She is asking Walden.

"By my boat."

"Where's your boat?"

"That's for me to know."

He steers me towards the door.

"For now."

- 7 7 -

He is fighting to remain composed in light of the fact that the old bag openly refuses to acknowledge his identity. He reminds himself that he is close to the finishing line, *Poor muddled Neil follows Ulster in angling for a conclusion (9,4)*, and that he cannot let her obstinacy get in the way of a glorious final sprint. He knows he cannot afford to unleash the full extent of his wrath if he is to have any hope of getting her on board the boat from which he longs to push her to her end, *New lair is final (3)*.

He will have to enlist Davina's help to get the job done, which means he will have to take them both fishing. Although this is not what he had intended, he can see there are some advantages. An alibi for one thing, should there be any trouble in the days immediately following the accident.

He is walking back the way he came, only this time he is walking with Davina who, he is happy to note, is enjoying holding his hand as much as he is enjoying having it there. He is tired now, after his nocturnal voyage and hours without sleep, but he does not let it show. She asks him if he knows where they're going, and he responds by asking her if he looks like the kind of father who comes this far without a solid plan.

James was as surprised to see Morna the second time she came to his hotel room as he had been the first. Perhaps even more so, for on the second occasion, she didn't even knock. Since her previous appearance less than half an hour earlier, he had showered and dressed his way through a dream sequence of the coming hours and days and, if he played his cards well, perhaps even years.

Firstly, he would do as Morna insisted, and get Ruth off the island. The only amendment he would make to her plan would be to take her with them as well. It might not amount to a riding into the sunset scenario, but he was not about to leave a pensioner to face the potential fate of being tied up in cat gut in the middle of the sea. Even if the victim, as he suspected she might be, were guilty of the crime levelled at her. He was spinning this thought into a vision of a late night years down the line, a night on which Morna was finally opening up about what Walden had done to sentence himself to a life in the cold, when the woman in question flung open his hotel room door.

"Back again? I was just thinking about you."

"He's got her."

"Who?"

"Ruth. Walden has got her. You have to help me find them before he hurts her."

Morna looked at him breathlessly, pleadingly, her eyes spilling anguish down her cheeks.

"I'm coming. Do you know where they are?"

"I know which way they went. He wanted her to help him prepare for a fishing trip he says he wants to take me on. I said I would go with them, but he wouldn't let me. Neither would she. I'm scared for her. God knows what he might do."

"I don't think he wants to hurt her."

"You don't know anything about him."

James put on his boots and ran out of the hotel as fast as Morna's lead would allow, her words turning on their axis of potential implication.

"Which way did they go?"

"I'll show you. You don't know the island."

"No, just tell me. I'll be faster than you."

"Towards the beach beside the Machair."

"Which way is that? Show me and I'll find them."

Morna pointed him in the direction she had seen Walden lead her daughter, and James started running. He crossed fields, followed tracks, combed the beach, and scrambled rocks, but it was not until he climbed onto the dunes and saw a dot moving slowly towards two distant islands, that he paused for breath. Though it was too far out for him to know for sure, he felt that he did, and that the dot was a boat containing a madman and the woman for whom he had come and fallen so far.

- 79 -

We're a long way from shore now and he still shows no sign of stopping. I want to tell him enough is enough and that we can turn back, but the set of his jaw and curl of his lip warn me to keep my peace. I replay the events that pushed me into the boat: his invitation; my polite refusal on the grounds that, like my mother, I'm afraid of both boats and deep water. His insistence that he's a good oarsman and that I need not be worried about either. My counter insistence that I would prefer to stay on dry ground. I can still hear him shouting that I should do what he says and not as my mother might, and I can still feel the force with which he gripped and steered me resolutely onto the wet seat upon which I am now sitting.

He is rowing, his back to the water, his face to me. He smiles. I try to reciprocate because out here, surrounded by cold deep water, anything else would be insane. I put my hand in the sea to allow something of me to become accustomed to the temperature into which I cannot help but think he is going to try and throw me.

"You see, the boat is fine. I told you there was nothing to fear, *Echo in distance causes fright (4)*."

He is mumbling to himself and I wonder why I did not jump out or refuse to get in while I still had the chance.

"It is not the boat I had in mind for us, but it can hold its own in a storm, and it will serve its purpose well enough."

He stops rowing and looks around, a smile touching the corners of his thin lips.

"This will do. No-one will disturb us here."

I nod my head in agreement, wishing for the very life of me that he were wrong. But there is no other boat anywhere. No tours, no fishermen, no ferries, not even so much as a fish in sight. Just Walden and I at sea with two rods and lines, which I know we are not about to cast out in order to catch our supper.

"Since your mother is so determined to pretend she doesn't know who I am, you are going to have to play a more decisive role in getting her both onto and off the boat."

I take my hand out of the water. It's numb.

"As you know, I wrote that she drowned trying to save me. That part remains unchanged. But we will have to be clever if we are to avoid a struggle."

He speaks his words as if they were describing the normal things that people do.

"You will sit right where you are now. Only perhaps you could be a little more cheerful. We don't want to give the game away."

I'm listening to him, but my mind is working as hard as it ever has to find a way out of this.

"I will stand up as if I have caught a large fish, and then I fall in. Once that happens, you have to encourage her to jump overboard to rescue me... Davina? You look so sad? You mustn't worry about me, my dear, I really am an excellent swimmer."

He reaches over to stroke my knee, and I am clenching my teeth and my fists as tight as I can to keep myself from crying, and him, this maniac, from seeing how I really feel about what he's telling me.

"If she doesn't jump, you have to push her. Then once she is in the water, I will duck her so her lungs start to fill with water. I will let her up, then duck her again, bit by bit, to make it look as authentic as possible."

Sobs are rising in me, but I cough them away. He must not know for, unlike him, I cannot claim to be a strong swimmer. I sit very still and let him talk.

"She's old and I daresay feeble, so it ought not take very long. Once she has given up the fight, we'll drag her into the boat and wrap her legs in fishing wire. And there we shall have poetic justice. Her drowning, *Medic having a watery end* (8), not mine. And after the funeral you and I can finally be together. Just the two of us. Nobody will ever come between us again."

A hopeful part of me is waiting for the punch line, for the "I'm only joking", but I know it isn't coming. Walden means it. He really thinks he is my father. He really wants me to push my mother out of this boat and spend the rest of his life with me cut off from the rest of the world. I can't look at him. I just hold my trembling knees and keep telling myself that if I play along, we'll get back to shore where James and my mother will be there with some help. As long as he doesn't decide to take me to his remote hideaway now, there is still a chance that this will end well.

"Any questions?"

He is standing in the boat and I clutch the sides as it rocks in response to his uneven footing.

"Davina, I asked if you have any questions?"

"No. I understand everything. Shall we go back in now?"

"Not before we have practiced. If your mother does not volunteer to jump in and save me, which is the least she owes me, you will, as I said, have to help her. She might resist and you don't want to capsize the whole boat, so you have to push her in the right way. One way is to grab her ankles, and you can do this without standing up yourself."

He is now standing in the middle of the boat, taking off his suit and shirt, and is beckoning to me to sit on the middle seat.

"Come on. You're not going to get much of a grip from there."

It takes me a moment to realise what he is suggesting, but when I do, I slowly move to sit next to him, my eyes now pinned to his.

"Good. Now, take hold of my ankles."

I do what he says.

"No. Not like that. That barely tickles. You have to really grab them, tight enough to tip her right over the edge."

My hands follow his instructions and the next thing I am aware of is the splash his body makes as it hits the water. For a second he is gone and I am hopeful that he will not surface, that the fish he wrote about will be there waiting to drag him to the deepest depths of this cold cold sea.

He bobs up near the front of the boat.

"Well done, you'll have her in in no time." He's laughing.

No I won't. Never.

"And once she's in, I'll take over. But like I said, there must be no evidence of a struggle. No clutching at the sides of the boat making a scene. So you must keep the boat out of her reach. Is that clear?"

"Yes."

My fingers are shaking uncontrollably as I wrap them around the oars. I lift them and pull them clumsily through the water.

"I'm not a very good rower."

"Then you must practice."

He is swimming towards the boat.

"The oars should enter the water blade down, as if they were slicing it, and when you pull them out, they must be flat."

As he speaks I am trying to row. I used to know how, but my muscles are so tense that there is no synchronicity to my movements. I dip too deep, then too shallow, my oars shuddering through the sea moving the boat in a circle, and me closer to him.

"Come on Davina, I'm sure you can do better than that. Blades down on impact. Both oars at the same time."

He is now treading water at the front of the boat and is reaching up to hold the side and, I fear, lift himself back in.

I slide the oars through the water, desperate to take this chance he has given me.

"Like this?"

I am two strokes away from him. But I need to be three, four, more, many many more.

"That's it. You're getting the idea. Keep going."

I follow his instructions, which take me another meter from him. If I keep going like this…

"Good girl. Well done. You won't need to get any further away from her than that."

He is now about five or six metres from me.

"You can stop now. I'm cold."

I don't stop. I won't stop. I slice the oars through the water, just as he told me to. Once, twice, three times. He is looking at me, shouting.

"I said stop."

I shake my head and keep rowing, pushing my arms to move faster. I glance behind me to the distant shore. It is a long way, but each stroke takes me a little closer to it. I can do this. I turn back to Walden, but he is gone. I slow down as I look around me for any sign of him. There is nothing. My heart thudding, I return to my rowing.

"What the hell are you doing?"

My scream is short and sharp, but my panic endless. He is only a metre away from the front of the boat, and is glaring at me.

"Stop this boat. That is an order, Davina Law."

I keep rowing, harder than ever before, but no matter how hard I row, he remains level with me. As if he is attached to the boat. He lifts one arm out of the water, and I see that he is. He is holding the rope tied to the front and I am pulling him with me. I don't know how to get him off. I can't move from where I am and wrestle him for the rope. I can't do anything except keep rowing.

"I don't like it when people disobey me, Davina. And I clearly told you to cease rowing."

His weight is slowing me down, making my arms ache, and he seems to be getting even closer to me.

"You can't get away from me."

But I can try. I can let all the fear and panic and loathing coursing through me give me whatever strength it is going to take to yank myself free of him. I row and I row until I hit my stride. If I keep going like this, I can at least prevent him from getting inside the boat. But I don't keep going. I catch a crab. I didn't know I remembered that term until this moment, until now, when I have had to stop rowing because the oar won't move. I recall it happening to me when I learnt to row, and from a forgotten place, I know what I have to do. I pull the oar in and over my head to reposition it. I do it as fast as I can, but it is not fast enough, because Walden is now holding on to the front of the boat, shaking his head.

"Stop the boat, Davina."

I don't look at him, except out of the tiniest corner of my eye. I am too afraid of what I will see. I row instead. I have to pick up pace again or he will be back inside, and then… I don't know what. I want to look behind me to see how much further we have to go, but I have to focus on the rowing, on getting it right.

"You will regret this disobedience."

He is clinging to the rim of the boat, and I can see him trying to climb over.

"No."

"No? You are saying 'no' to me?"

I can't speak. I can't do anything except move this boat through the water. We're going faster again, too fast for him to do anything other than cling on. But one more mistake… I can see help and danger approaching. A wave. A big one is coming towards us. Walden is blind to it, but I can tell it is going to hit him. It is going to hit both of us. I watch it carefully and at the very last moment, stop rowing and pull in the oars, clutching them for dear life.

I bounce through the wave, salt water drenching me and sloshing into the bottom of the boat. I am still afloat. I put the oars back out, scouting around for Walden at the same time. He has vanished from sight. I daren't hope that we have been separated, just as I daren't look behind me for fear that he will be there. Climbing into the boat.

"Davina!"

I look to my left, and there he is. Close, but not close enough. And then I see the rope, held by nothing but the water in which it trails. I row for less than a minute, then let go of the oars and carefully move to the front of the boat to pull the rope inside. I look at Walden all the while, as if my eyes will keep him at a safe distance.

"Come and get me, Davina."

I'm back at the oars.

"I said come and get me."

"My name is Ruth."

"Come back."

I don't respond. I need every bit of energy and concentration to get to shore.

"Davina! You will come back here right now. Right now."

I row and row and row in the direction my body tells me is home. I don't look to make sure, because I can't take my eyes off him for fear that he might suddenly catch up with me. He is still moving towards me, and I recall his words about being a strong swimmer.

"You will not leave me here."

I will.

"Davinaaaaaa!"

I am going faster now, and with each stroke he grows smaller and smaller. I know what is happening and that I'm responsible for the growing gulf between us, yet I am barely conscious of having created it. I keep going, slicing through the water until he has faded to almost nothing but a voice, a voice which is still shouting the name that isn't even mine.

- 80 -

He is swimming as hard as he can, but the water is cold and he is tired. He is choleric, yet cannot give his feelings a vent without running the risk of swallowing water. He does not like salt on his food, and even less in his fluids, so he keeps his mouth closed and allows his mounting panic to decide his course of action.

He knows he does not stand a chance of catching up with the boat she is rowing away with such determination. He has two choices. He can hedge his bets and try to swim back to Iona where he now has two scores to settle, or he can swim to one of the islands behind him, which are closer, but still an exhausting distance away.

He is deliberating when he first notices the clouds moving in and the water rising. He might have been able to weather a storm from within the now distant vessel but, cast from it, he doesn't stand such a strong chance. The odds are now on as to whether he is going to live, *Wire that could shock you (4),* or die, *No victory in dive is terminal (3).* He wants to live, *Four exist in French article (4),* and not die, *Strange Ide is Roman day (3).* He therefore launches himself in the direction the tide is taking him, back to Iona, *In the seraglio Nathan seeks a Scottish woman (4).*

He will have to swim fast if he is to reach rather than be washed up on its shores, and he relays the message to every muscle, sinew, and tendon in his body. This, he tells them, is their chance to prove their superiority over his otherwise unbeatable brain. He will, he promises them, reward their efforts with whatever they want, if only they can get him there.

- 8 1 -

The waves are getting up, and they petrify me. I'm far enough away from him now to turn round and judge my distance from the shore. In my mind it's right behind me. Just a few metres away.

A backwards glance shows me I am not as close as I wish, but closer than Walden, and close enough to see small figures moving along the beach. The water is vast and as terrifying as the man I left in it, but it seems to be on my side. The tide is carrying me home. I row with it. I row for my life, for my mother's life.

I've heard people say that to drown is to see your life flash before you. I'm not drowning, but I see my life. I see my summers, so far from deprived, spent on the beach towards which I'm now headed, I see my mother standing behind me, watching my every move, but always distant, always wary of me. I see myself leaving home to get away from her and the difficulty of being her daughter. I see the isolation I found in my new home, I see my own difficulties of simply being, my failure to be anything more than my mother's fear, my mother's distance and wariness of me, and I understand. I understand everything.

I hear shouting on the beach, sent by the wind to draw me home. I am coming. I am coming home. I think of what my life could have been, and of what it still might. I think of Hazel and of Paul, who I instinctively know I will never see again.

The voices are getting louder, but not loud enough for me to recognise them or what they're saying. I want them to belong to my mother and Jim. I conjure an image of them on the shore, spurring me on, but it is infused with the final words of Walden's book.

> *...she would want for nothing and no-one, because she would have him. And with him, she would do what all good books promise, in that she would live happily ever after.*

I would not have been happy Mr Walden, Mr Ned Law. And neither would you. Your ruthlessness would never have allowed it. I am thinking of what I will tell any-one who might want to know what happened to him. I will not tell them of my own ruthlessness, but of a tragic acci-dent. Of a visitor to the island who wanted to go boating, and who insisted on going for a swim, only to be swept away by a gathering storm.

It is them. I can hear them both shouting my name. My real name. I turn around to see James in the water just a few feet away. He is up to his knees and waiting to pull the boat ashore. I row towards him, and let him help me out. I would like to fall into his arms, to drown in the safety they would surely offer, but standing behind them is my real protector. There is my mother. I walk towards her.

- 8 2 -

He is doing well. He has established a rhythm and is recit-
ing "she loves me, she loves me not" as he moves up and
down with the waves. He decides she does not, and that he
does not care. He never wanted her for love. He just wanted
what belonged to him.

He is hit by a big wave and, for a moment, is forced far
beneath the surface of the water. He does not like it down
there and when he emerges it is to the sight of a lightning
bolt shocking the sky. He counts the seconds until the first
thunder, *Clap to rend hut differently (7)*. It is nineteen,
which he divides by five to establish that the storm is 3.8
miles from him. He does not have 3.8 miles left to travel to
reach his destination, but the storm is moving faster than
him, and is slowing him down. And he is cold. Colder than
he has ever been.

He can no longer see her boat, or any other. He sees
nothing and nobody. He is alone. Alone at sea. He is in
trouble, *First part of East End wife? (7)*. Oh yes, and grave
trouble at that.

He is pushed under by another big breaker. He comes
up spluttering and treads water while he regains his numb
composure and gathers enough energy to keep going. He
has survived worse, and he will survive this. But the storm
is coming closer, and is working the waves into a frenzy.
They have located him now and they are not going to let
him out of their sights. He is surging forth to escape them,
but they are everywhere around him. *No victory in dive is
terminal (3)*.

He is swallowing water, too much to be good for him. With each mouthful, he becomes more disoriented. His will to survive is keeping him afloat, his panic dragging him down. He sees her before him. He sees her on the train. Not her, but her. Shelagh. So many years ago, same red hair. Like mother like daughter. He did not love her. He does not believe in love. He believes in ownership, and she is his. She consented to that in the house she regards as holy. He sees her face. He is stroking it, then hitting it. Hard and harder. He sees her holding the baby. The baby is crying. It will not stop crying. He sees himself lash out as he was taught to do. And he smiles.

Crossword Solutions

Chapter 3

Medical verdict when spotless William removes nothing from the loofah mix (5, 3, 2, 6) – CLEAN BILL OF HEALTH

Eternity in a cod for example - that's a few degrees over (8) - FEVERISH

Nothing to link gas and linear measures in this mercurial device (11) - THERMOMETER

Poorly like a Venetian boss who's lost his bottom? Or just plain fed up? (4, 2, 1, 3) – SICK AS A DOG

Public land which is rarely warm. It's viral! (6, 4) – COMMON COLD

Chapter 7

Mayfair, or thereabouts, north east. Vintage stuff! (4) - WINE

Blooms as distinguished chap hides German lion? (7) - FLOWERS

New couple at it, indeed (8) - COPULATE

After some gym Romeo adds gas to make present for a lady? (7) – RO-MANCE

Chapter 9

Long-term commitment to spoil one before mixing five hundred I feel (7, 4) - MARRIED LIFE

Joining together in a Berlin suburb (7) - WEDDING

All promises as Robert the old pop idol makes painful cries (4) - VOWS

Small jumper in genetically modified state makes for a stable person (5) - GROOM

Make Waldo bring a special dress (6, 4) - BRIDAL GOWN

Chapter 12

Spry Leo deranged by affliction (7) - LEPROSY

Les, our cubist becomes all-consuming (12) – TUBERCULOSIS

Chapter 14

Some French have very small following, but make a lot (7) - DESTINY

Unexpected outcome is put off after cards are dealt then consumed (4,2,4) - HAND OF FATE

Driving aid and famous Moabite are incontestable (5) – TRUTH

Chapter 16

Fifty in a sandy place provide germ killer (6) - BLEACH

Detectives tail older person to cleaner? (4) - SOAP

Mutated shrub after single wormwood and a Christmas crooner provide a means to shift the dirt (9,5) - SCRUBBING BRUSH

Backward Brit down under has some head of hair! (3) - MOP

Essential to life of revolting peasant and reigning monarch (5) – WATER

Chapter 23

Reflects that daily one is mostly black and white (6) - MIRROR

He contains order of merit at his house (4) - HOME

French go south east to hold flowers (4) - VASE

Where and on what Othello goes back to sleep (7) – BEDROOM

Chapter 29

No pen pot! One to contest perhaps? (8) – OPPONENT

Active conflict brings air force back in Hertfordshire town (7) – WAR-FARE

Antagonist got me mixed up in Japanese currency deal (5) - ENEMY

Prisoner and French cop tango – but don't see eye to eye (8) – CONFLICT

Chapter 32

Such endless organized religion meets Gestapo to fulfil objective (7) – SUCCESS

Mechanical herald in great victory (7) – TRIUMPH

Search after trick to vanquish the foe (8) - CONQUEST

A Companion of Honour that is, without His Excellency, vehement in claiming result – ACHIEVEMENT (11)

Chapter 35

New pears paid for but no longer visible (9) – DISAPPEAR

Can't be seen in caravan I share (6) – VANISH

Departed for Geordieland after his turn (4) – GONE

Youngster slept while taken. (9) – KIDNAPPED

Chapter 45

Foxtrot to the lavatory backwards? What an idiot! (4) – FOOL

Just stupidity to think half diode would work in such a cold state - (6) – IDIOCY

Takes a numbskull to heed a good French word! (8) - BONEHEAD

Chapter 51

Beguiled, besotted or just below the table? (5, 3, 9) - UNDER THE IN-FLUENCE

Destroyed potato within, but in Latin! (7) – SMASHED

Spirit found in child's bed in south Switzerland (6) – SCOTCH

Confused Kurd ran after dog initially – he's the worse for wear (8) – DRUNKARD

Chapter 57

Life draining event reversed about and after muddled percussion (6) - MURDER

Imperial measure back to replace small fish's head at this bash (8) - BLUDGEON

Distorted and wrung in hand before being billeted as severe punishment (4, 5, 3, 9) – HUNG, DRAWN AND QUARTERED

Chapter 61

No ace in this vast wet expanse (5) – OCEAN

Giant in charge of sinking ship (7) – TITANIC

Zebra angry with Dutch bank (8) – CROSSING

Travel for a day in France with Napoleonic marshal (7) - JOURNEY

Chapter 63

Draw back after commanding officer finds one with fear (6) – COWARD

Felix is frightened perhaps (7, 3) – SCAREDY CAT

Echo in distance causes fright (4) - FEAR

Apprehension comes from shaking tepid ration (11) – TREPIDATION

Chapter 67

Spirit is shaken at end of epoch - or just time passing by (5) – AGEING

So, few years are in you then? (5) – YOUTH

Chapter 71

Mythical singleton sees red (4) - FURY

Cross ghostly figure with no eye to make Scottish outerwear? (5) - WRATH

Sun god needs power company added to show off his anger (4) - RAGE

One's mood deteriorates in frying rump steak (5) - GRUMP

Is Di tanning - or just affronted (9) – INDIGNANT

Chapter 73

Gritty new conjunctions! (4) – SAND

Alternative within her beside the seaside (5) – SHORE

Odd bottle stoppers seem stony! (5) – ROCKS

Where muddled oafs may sit (4) - SOFA

Chapter 77

New lair is final (3) – END

Poor muddled Neil follows Ulster in angling for a conclusion (9,4) - FINISHING LINE

Chapter 80

Wire that could shock you (4) – LIVE

No victory in dive is terminal (3) – DIE

Four exist in French article (4) – LIVE

Strange Ide is Roman day (3) – DIE

In the seraglio Nathan seeks a Scottish woman (4) – IONA

Chapter 82

Clap to rend hut differently (7) - THUNDER

First part of East End wife? (7) - TROUBLE

TAMSIN WALKER

Tamsin Walker was raised in Yorkshire, England and studied at the National Academy of Writing (NAW). Her short fiction has been published in several anthologies and her plays have been performed in the UK and Germany. Her short plays *Indecent Exposure* and *Digits* won competitions at the English Theatre Berlin and Bristol's Tobacco Factory respectively.

She works as a journalist in Berlin, where she also writes a regular radio column for DW, Germany's international broadcaster, on the quirks and perks of life in her long-time adopted home. She has five children.

Impersonation is her debut novel.

www.tamsinkwalker.co.uk